The Path to

Psychosis

by

Charles Riffle

Table of Contents

The First Cut………………………………………………… 3

Pain Redefined……………………………………………… 5

Dying Eyes…………………………………………………. 60

Watching……………………………………………………. 93

The Devil Walking Next to Me…………………………… 95

Trick or Treat…………………………………………….. 120

Rosie……………………………………………………….. 137

My Brother Phil…………………………………………... 167

USA Husbands…………………………………………….,. 168

The Tree at the Top of the Hill…………………………... 204

The Bad Daddy…………………………………………….. 215

Excerpt: Agnes of Death…………………………………… 246

The First Cut

He stood there looking at the man tied to the chair wondering to himself with a kind of excitement "Is it going to happen this time? Am I really going to do this?"

In his early thirties now, he had been dreaming of this moment since he was 14. That is when he had seen his first slasher movie. It opened up such emotions for him. That want and need to kill. He had planned it out for so many years even going as far as stalking potential first victims but he would always relent just before he was about to make his move. Taking this man was easy though; he had come from a local pub and was very inebriated.

The basement was dark and dirty. A typical basement, a washer and dryer set to the side, a weight bench, several plastic storage containers and an area with various tools. There was one window with a thick, dirty tan curtain over it.

"Please man. Don't do this." The man tied to the chair said. "I have a family."

The stranger just looked at him with slight confusion. "I had a family once." He said in a slow and very cold tone. "Doesn't everyone have a family at some point?"

In reality, he had only had a family at birth and never knew nor wanted to know who they were. He was bounced around between the orphanage and different foster homes when the foster family felt his uncaring and cold manner were getting to be too much for them. He was never a bad child, never got in to trouble and never hurt a living being despite his desires.

He stood there for a moment wondering what it would be like to feel sympathy for this man. Would he feel remorse for killing him? Will he be satisfied with just one kill?

He was sweating now and his hands were shaky. This was the closest he had come to fulfilling what he felt was his destiny. He knew it was now or never. With that thought he plunged the knife forward.

Pain Redefined

Chapter 1:

Julie Proctor

"How much does one really know about one's self until they

explore the threshold of their pain?" That's the answer I always give

to my victims when they ask me the question "Why?", and they

always ask the question. And while we're on the subject I don't like

to use the word victim. I like to call them the "Free". Victim is the

word the police and the media like to use. You may call my mind

twisted, and I'm sure you will by the end of my story, but I will tell

you that I believe I am doing an invaluable service to the "Free".

Before they have passed and I have laid them to rest, releasing them

from this beyond cruel world, they get to explore a side of

themselves that they never knew existed. Giving them a chance to feel that physical pain and torment sets their minds free and allows them to truly live if even for only a short time.

My name is totally unimportant to this story. What matters is my work. The "Free" are specially researched and chosen. I research their background, trying to figure out what is truly on their inside, not the inside that I physically show them but the true inner emotional, mental workings of their soul. My "Free" have to possess certain characteristics. A weak moral fiber for example, which includes a total disregard for their fellow man, an ability to know right from wrong, but choosing to ignore it and most importantly an ability to love, but the stubborn nature to not allow themselves to.

Those are qualities that my first "Free" subject possessed. Someone I truly loved, but who refused to give in to her love for me. Her name was Julie Proctor. I remember the first time I saw Julie. She was standing by a tree near the entrance of my place of work. Her hair was a beautiful shoulder length blonde. She looked in my direction and smiled with such pearly white teeth. I wanted to talk to her but did not feel like I could even approach her let alone talk to her but I knew if I didn't I would not get another chance. I slowly walked her way, not quite sure what I was about to say. Should I be flirty? Or should I just start a casual conversation and hope that she finds me interesting enough to want to talk to again? I ended up going with a combination of both.

"This must be my lucky day." I proclaimed as I got as close as I could to her without being instantly labeled as creepy.

"I'm sorry?" She said, looking slightly bemused, but still with a fractional grin on her face.

"I said: This must be my lucky day." I went on to explicate. "I had a lovely day at work, and as soon as I step outside I see that it's a lovely day and there is a lovely lady standing out here."

Now I think I should make it plain that at this juncture I had never even thought of killing anyone, or as I like to say setting them free. I had an average childhood. I was never bullied in school. I was never molested by my parents, an elder uncle or the priest at the church I attended growing up. Years from now when someone is looking at my background and trying to puzzle out what made me into a killer, as they will call it, I'm sure, they will not find anything to support their clichéd impression that I became what I am because of an atrocious life I had as a child. I, in reality, had a very great upbringing. My parents were extraordinary and I still have a wonderful family relationship with them, I was always at the top of my class in school and I have always had at least three or four close friends.

"Aren't you charming?" she said with a vast smile on her face. Her blue eyes were melting me at this point. "My name is Julie."

I told her my name and caught myself agaze a little too much so I looked away. "This may be a little forward and sudden, but if you are not too engaged would you like to get a cup of coffee or something with me?" I asked, disquieted that I had asked too soon.

"I don't see why not. You seem harmless enough." She said with a tenuous titter.

We walked to a diner a couple blocks away. We sat and talked for hours. I learned more about her in that time than I think I have ever known about any one. She told me about her mother and father, her first cat, her occupation, her apartment and all of its ruination. She was not a wealthy lady by any standards but that did not concern her because she was blissful with her place in life.

We spent the night together and it was without a doubt the best sexual experience I had ever had. At one point I almost caught myself shrieking with delight. I was wholly certain that after that night I was utterly and completely in love. Who would not have been in love after such a night of conversation and mutuality of your innermost feelings with another followed by hours of fervent love making?

A major part of me still loves Julie to this day even though it's impossible to be with her since she is the inaugural member of the "Free". She really showed me how to truly live in a lot of ways. I could have never loved anyone the way I loved her and I could have never tested the threshold of my emotional pain without her. Julie was really where my life began.

Over the next two weeks everything was grand. We spent most of our leisure time together talking and making love. However, after those two weeks something changed.

"I don't think we're ready for meeting each other's parents." She said as I felt my heart sink into a vast oblivion.

"Why not, my love?" I asked, terrified at her response.

"That seems like a relationship thing." And there it was. Was I really that narrow minded? We hadn't known each other for long, but surely the quality of time outweighed the quantity of time.

I looked into her eyes, not quite sure how to select my next words. So I blurted out the first words that came to me.

"I thought this was a relationship."

"It's been a really great couple of weeks, but I'm not sure I'm ready to put a label on this." She verbalized.

I could not conceive of what I was hearing. I frankly thought we were in love. I wondered if I had not bestowed on it the proper amount of time. Maybe I was erroneous in my haste. Perhaps I should just see how things progress over the next month or so.

"I think I need to take a step back and see if this is really what I want." She professed quite heartlessly.

"You do not want to see me any longer?" I asked, trying to battle back the mist in my eyes.

"I'm not saying that. I enjoy our time together…" she "enjoys" our time together? "But I think we moved a little too fast."

You should have thought about that before you laid down on my bed and spread your legs before me, I wanted to state. But all I managed to mutter was: "If space is what you wish then space is what I shall give you."

In fact, I really did not give her said space. I called her many times over the next few days, becoming overly acquainted with her voicemail. I watched her as well. I had actually appropriated a few sick days from work just to do as such. Having a doctor for a friend is quite convenient at times.

On our fourth day divided something inexcusable occurred. I saw her going into the diner, where we shared our archetypal evening together, with another man, a very well-favored man at that. I watched them at the diner. They were there for an hour before they retired to his home.

She decided coitus with this trespasser to our relationship was logical. This hurt worse than any physical pain I had felt or could ever dispense to anyone. I stood outside the window for what seemed like an eternity.

I cried that night, as if a punished child might, until I fell asleep. I awoke the next morning feeling something unexpected. I felt refreshed, a calm sense about me. Julie had hurt me in the worst way imaginable, but I had survived it. I felt no anger towards her. I was still feeling the pain but I was adjusted. The pain had opened my eyes.

I realized Julie did not quite understand what she had thrown away. Someone allegiant, devoted to her and loving her unconditionally. It was not her fault. It was how her life had played out to this point. I knew what I had to do. I had to show her how to live and then I had to set her "Free".

I entered her apartment as she slept. I used a chloroform drenched rag to help her stay dormant. The chloroform, which I had taken from my place of occupation, would be useful in my future "Free" work. I fastened her, entirely unclothed, to the coffee table in her living room. The table was not large and I am sure very uncomfortable.

I made the first cut just above her belly button. It was exhilarating. She stirred her body as much as she could, considering she was tied down so firmly. I know she wanted to scream with ecstasy but the gag in her mouth forbid it.

"I hope this makes you understand how much I love you." I told her as I was fashioning my third cut across her left breast. "You need to experience this pain in order to feel life. I forgive you for your tryst with another man. I realize now that I just needed to work more diligently on our relationship and I am confident that just before you take your parting breath, you will love me like you could have never loved another."

I worked on her for two days. I was so young and immature. Some cuts I made weren't deep enough and brought forth very little blood. I was quite sloppy with her and I feel dreadful about that to this day. I should have taken more time with her particularly in the last moment as I made the final cut across her tubular cavity, severing her jugular.

"Sleep well my love. I shall be with you for eternity one day, but for now, I have much work to do." I said after she had expired.

I am sure she understood the intent and hopefully she realized that she was my fate. She was meant to enter my life to force me to perceive how to live and to spread that life into others. I showed her actual pain for the first time in her 20 years on this earth.

I had never felt so alive, so accomplished as I had after I had set Julie "Free". In her last few breaths I saw a look in her eyes. I knew she wanted to say "Thank you."

Chapter 2

Doug Spencer

I have decided not to go in any particular order or to reference everyone I have set "Free". That would take far too long. I am only going to mention those that were extraordinary to me for diverse reasons.

My second kill, for instance, was not my top-quality work by any means and decidedly far too effortless. She was a cocotte whose name I had never learned. I kept her in my basement for days. She was, for the most part, an experimentation. I recall how she squirmed as I inserted the sewing needles into her breasts as if they were sizable pin cushions. The needles remained there until I set her "Free."

She, like a few other of the females I had taken, offered me sexual favors in transaction for their life. I am ashamed to admit that I took them up on their offers in the beginning until I really converged with my higher purpose. In retrospect, I was not being untruthful with them when I was saying I would accept the favors and let them live. Because they did live, and I mean truly live, just before I set them "Free." After a few times I realized how weak they were to offer these sexual trades to me and how weak I was to accept them. I can assure you though I punished myself well for these transgressions. Acid taken from the place of my occupation was enough to make sure I stayed on the straight and narrow.

The next "Free" I would like to talk about is Doug Spencer. He is special because as much as I adored Julie, conversely, I hated Doug with just as much passion. Doug taught me a lesson, however, and that is that I should have no emotions towards my "Free." I should not love, hate or have emotion whatsoever towards someone I have decided to set "Free." I should only focus on my calling. However, this is easier said than practiced.

Doug was a simple person to get acquainted with, as I would learn. All that was required for that task was a considerable amount of alcohol. I really could not believe the things he told me, a sheer stranger, on this fateful night.

"… So I shoved the money in my pocket, closed the drawer and got the hell out of there." He continued before taking yet another helping of his beer, of which he had partaken several at this point. He had been talking incessantly about the time he walked in to his boss's office, when he was not there, going through his desk drawers, discovering his petty cash and ultimately determining he should keep the money.

This watering hole I had followed him into was very dark and had a dampish state. Like that of a basement. The basement in my home upon which I would take my "Free" for their lessons was much like this bar, very dark and algid. I believe it lends to the experience. If it was bright and comfortable it would make them feel too at home and should not, having no comforts be a part of their experience?

"So, buddy, are you married? Any children?" He asked, obviously trying to keep the conversation going.

"No. Never had the opportunity."

"Lucky guy, I have been married for eight years and I have two kids. It's a real pain in the ass. My kids are brats and my wife is a prude. Never wanting to try anything different in the bedroom, never wants to have a drink and always complains because I want to drink beer and watch football on the weekend. Getting married was my worst mistake." He drank about half of his beer before finishing. "I taught her though." He leaned closer as if to tell some profound secret, but I knew in my mind what he was about to say. "She gets too mouthy and I put her in her place. Usually just a back hand, but a good solid fist when necessary. I put her in the hospital for a few days once."

He was actually bragging at this juncture. I wanted to end him here and now. I detested him before this revelation. I hated him more now and I would hate him more by the end of the night.

We left the bar together conversing as we walked towards his car, where he was, undoubtedly, about to drive off inebriated, if it wasn't for the reality that I was about to make him a member of the "Free."

I have never been the best conversationalist, but I managed to keep a dialogue going with Doug. I needed to stall so I could figure a way to lure him to my house. Then he made another revelation. One that I already knew, but was taken aback to hear nonetheless.

"Can you keep a secret?" He asked.

"Sure." I said, with my sub-par conversation skills.

"A few months ago I met up with this chick I had been talking to online for a while…"

"Let me guess… She had a penis." I said jestingly, but really just delaying the inevitable.

"No man." He said with a slight smile. "Let me finish. So I had been talking to this chick, but I couldn't meet her for a while because of my wife and kids always being around. So my wife takes the kids to her parents place for a few days. I told her we should meet. We meet and let me tell you this chick is hot! We go back to my place and just fuck all night long. So after this she keeps calling me for days. Saying she loves me and shit, wanting me to leave my wife."

"What did you tell her?" I asked through gritted teeth.

"I told her to fuck off. I wasn't going to leave my wife. She would take me for everything I ever earned. But this stupid chick kept calling me for a few days after that, and then the phone calls suddenly stopped. I saw her on the news a day or two later, somebody killed her. They sliced her up pretty bad. Can you believe my luck? She could have ruined me." He laughed. "But somebody offed her." He continued his story "I'm pretty sure it was this weirdo she said was bothering her. He was in love with her, but she just wanted to be his friend." I am pretty sure I visibly winced at his statement. "Only problem is I'm afraid someone will come forward and say they saw us together. That could ruin everything for me. I should have never messed with that crazy bitch."

"I don't think you will have to worry about it." I could not take any more.

"Why not?" He asked, looking bewildered.

"Because I'm going to set you Free." I had been, in fact, slipping the chloroform induced rag from the baggie in my pocket as he was closing his story.

He did not go down without a fight. Doug was a pretty large man. He slammed me against the wall and then to the ground. I had almost lost my grip on the rag, but just before I did the vapors from the chloroform overtook Doug Spencer.

I struggled getting him in my house just as I had struggled getting him in to my car. I was fortunate enough to have neighbors who were not prying and fortunate enough to have a driveway that went nearly to my basement door. As I struggled with the dead weight of this blithering jerk's body all I could evaluate was what I wanted to do to him. He was truly different from the other "Free", as much as I hate to acknowledge it, this was the only one I had set "Free" that I took pleasure in teaching. I would also be doing a favor to his wife and kids, ultimately. They deserved better, anybody deserved better than this cretin.

His first words upon waking were "What the fuck man?" Such eloquent colloquy.

"Why, whatever do you mean Mr. Spencer?" I asked sarcastically.

"Why am I tied to this God damn table naked!?" He shouted.

"You are part of a project I have started." I continued. "I am going to show you how to live through tremendous amounts of physical pain."

"What? Why me?" He asked, growing more concerned.

"People like you go through life taking and doing as you wish. You take money that is not yours, you maltreat your wife, you are unfaithful to your wife and above all you intruded into the wrong person's relationship. Yet you have no declination and you face no consequences. I'm going to reform you, show you how to live then, as I said before, set you "Free." I was aggravated. I wanted to blurt out some choice expletives even though I had not since I was 9 years old. My mother had smacked me in the face so hard that day that my mouth bled for hours.

"Wait… you're that creepy guy that was stalking Julie aren't you?" Did he really say that? Did this addlepated Neanderthal really call me "that creepy guy"? "She didn't love you, man. She was just a friend. She was going to change her number so you couldn't call her anymore."

"Julie and I were in love until you came along and ruined it." I said angrily.

"She would have never slept with you. She thought you were too weird to go out with."

"Julie and I made love many times." I yelled. I knew what was happening now I was lessening to his level. He was winning this round.

"You're crazy. She was in love with me." After he said that I really wanted to cause him pain.

"Your first lesson, Mr. Spencer, is never argue with a man holding a hammer, especially when you are defenseless." At that point I went to work on him, hitting him with immense force, using the hammer to produce my ire. I hit him in the chest a few times very hard. I hit him on both arms and both knees. I could not bring myself to halt, though I was not ready to set him "Free," as there was still so much work to do. My last hit was a smash to his scrotum, which caused him to turn his head enough to projectile vomit on the floor. This made me nauseous. I left him, letting him reflect upon the time I had just spent with him. I felt we had bonded. I had seen a new side of him, a side that reacted to pain with such displeasure. Yes, indeed, I liked this side of Doug Spencer.

I returned after several hours. He looked weary and beaten. Well… literally he had been beaten, but mentally and emotionally he looked beaten. That was good, now my real work could begin.

He looked slowly towards me and spoke through tears "Please… no more. Do you want money? I have a lot of money. I can get you as much as you want. I beg you. I have a wife and kids."

I almost laughed at that statement. If I did not know the situation I may have been tempted to let him go back to his family. But, unfortunately for him, I knew.

"I know you do not care for your wife or kids, you told me as much last night."

"What do you want then? Do you want me to say I'm sorry? Fine. I'm sorry." He yelled and then started getting enraged. "Let me go you son of a bitch. I swear I'll kill you when I get out of here." Did he think he was going to leave here? Not until my work was accomplished.

"I hope you enjoyed that Mr. Spencer because they were the last words you will ever speak." With that I abstracted the knife from my pocket and retrieved his tongue, not without a fight however. He bit me ferociously. The "Free" never quite understood until the final instant that I was doing them a justice. They would fight and curse and spit, but in the end they were primed to be "Free."

I spent several days with Doug. Experimenting with him, slicing across his chest and stomach, removing all of his fingers and toes. I bestowed a few bodily organs to his viewing pleasure. What I enjoyed the most was the manhood that he had seen so fit as to place inside Julie. It was a major adrenaline rush for me. I learned more about Doug without him being able to speak than I ever could have through a conversation.

At that moment that I had decided to finally set him "Free," I had forgiven Doug Spencer. I let go all the pain and anguish he caused me. I let go him coming in between my relationship with Julie. I discharged him from that burden and I released myself from my inner turmoil. I was, however, furious and discomfited in myself. I had let my emotions get in the way of my purpose. I had to be chastened. I swung the hammer at my knee almost instinctively. The rush of pain sent me to the floor. It hurt, but I had to learn.

After a few weeks I had nearly entirely physically cured and mentally I was once again focused. Someone like Doug Spencer would never again intrude on my life, my mind or most significantly my life's work. I knew modifications needed to be made. I needed to select my "Free" better. I needed to know more about them in order to serve them better.

From what I had heard they never found Doug Spencer's body. I watched his wife for a while. Even though she appeared gloomy at her husband's inauspicious disappearance I could tell she was relieved. I became slightly acquainted with her through a "chance" meeting at a supermarket. She is truly a sweet lady. She inquired about my limp.

"Oh it was my own doing. Always hurting myself." I said with a facial gesture.

Chapter 3

Diana Langley

I have never been fond of the term "cougar" but for all intents and purposes Diana Langley was a cougar. This, however, was not the reason I realized she needed to be set "Free."

Diana was a very captivating lady. At 45 she was more comely than any of the 20 somethings whom I also worked with. She had lengthy dark hair stood about 5'8 and had an endearing smile, which is an attribute I adore from the opposite sex. Diana had been attempting to court me since I began working with her. I was not preoccupied with her being much elder than I. I was not even genuinely solicitous about her promiscuity, which principally concerned much younger men. I was concerned with her disregard to my assertion of loving another. This also is not the rational motive to which I had decided to set her "Free".

I had begun to do research on Miss Langley one day and ascertained quite a bit about her. She had never been wedded. She had been an exotic dancer on several occasions in her earlier days. She had several unpaid parking tickets, which is neither here nor there. She lived in a very luxurious home, from what I had seen from the outside included an in ground pool with a deck and hot tub. For certain more than her salary could supply. Diana Langley had gone through life never allowing herself to feel real love, or consequently, allowing another to love her.

Essentially, she had never rightfully lived. She had never opened her mind or her heart to life. She had only selected to live a free life with no consequences. I could not stand by and let that come about. She would have to be taught a lesson, and then set "Free". Diana would be my first to have no affectional attachment with. I could concentrate on her. Teach her through pain what living is truly about. This time I would have to do something exceptional.

I decided I would have to become more intimately acquainted with Miss Langley. I would have to learn more about her so I would be able to serve her better. .

"Haven't I told you before to call me Diana?" She aforementioned with a smile. The skirt she was wearing was slit nearly up to her derriere. I could tell by her body language that she knew what I was thinking. More than probable she would not be able to fathom the ways I would punish myself for having these thoughts.

"Yes Diana. I do apologize." I said.

"I'll forgive you this time cutie." She said with a cordial smile. "What brings you to my neck of the woods today?

"I was just strolling through the hallways when I noticed you moving these rather large boxes and thought you may require some assistance." I said sheepishly.

"I would love help from such a strong young man." She said. I did enjoy her smile.

We moved the boxes for almost an hour's time. In that time I learned a little about Miss Langley. The most interesting of which was an inherent fear of snakes. This was something I would have to take into consideration. Fear and pain go hand in hand after all and snakes can cause as much pain as they cause fear.

"Would you like to come over for dinner Friday night?" Was the question she posed.

"That would be nice Miss... I mean Diana." I had turned her down on this offering many times before so her astonished expression was not inconspicuous. I had to accept her offering this time as it would be the consummate moment to go to work on Miss Langley.

During my few days before my time with Miss Langley I found two large *agkistrodon contortrix* snakes, commonly known as the copperhead, in the area behind my house. They were beautiful creatures and would serve me well in my lesson with Miss Langley.

I arrived at her home approximately 8pm that Friday evening. She was looking very lovely wearing a short, sleeveless red dress and coordinated high heels. I was already troubled that I was going to relish the evening a little too much.

"Come on in handsome. Dinner will be ready soon." She said as she took my jacket.

Despite my disliking for most home cooking. I genuinely enjoyed the country fried steak and mashed potatoes she had prepared. Later as we sat on her couch and conversed she revealed that a young man, who was apparently very wealthy due to a large inheritance who was also at least twenty years her junior and hopelessly in love with her had not only purchased this home for her but was also paying her utilities, her automobile lease payments, not to cite keeping her supply of non-prescription narcotics everlasting. Miss Langley was either not worried about or forgetting the concept that I could have her tested for drug use as I was technically one of her supervisors at work.

As we sat there talking she moved closer to me little by little. She began to unfasten my trousers and I almost panicked.

"Why do you have so many scars here darling?" She asked.

"Just... a little mishap a few years ago." I stumbled through these words. I never intended for any other female besides Julie to see this component of me again but despite knowing I was going to have to punish myself later I could not bring forward myself to stop Miss Langley from doing what she was about to do.

"It's okay baby. I will be gentle with you." She said before taking me into her oral fissure. I did not want to enjoy this but, as a heterosexual male, I could not mask my ecstasy.

"You realize this makes you mine, right?" She said, midway through the task she had taken upon herself. This statement brought me back to reality. I had told her numerous times before that I belonged to another but still she insisted upon trying to take me away from that love. She was no more reputable than Doug Spencer. I was going to let her finish what she was doing but instantly afterward I must begin my work showing her the way to live and then I would set her "Free".

I utilized my time in between rushes of pleasure wisely. I reached into my pocket for the zip lock bag containing a chloroform soaked rag. As she emptied her mouth I immediately put the rag to her face. She endeavored only somewhat before letting go.

She awoke two hours later, in my basement, tied up and in the nude. I had placed her flat inside a box I had constructed only the day before.

"My God... What is this? What are you doing?" She asked though still in a stupor.

"I have done some research on you Miss Langley... Oh I'm sorry I should say Diana. I know that you require my help."

"What are you talking about?" She asked. There was no smile there any longer and that was an ignominy. That meant she truly did not understand the grandeur of this situation.

"I am going to show you how to live and I mean truly live. Then I will set you 'Free'." I answered.

"Please... Just set me free now... Please don't do whatever you are thinking about doing." She said through tears.

"That would be of no help to you. You do not realize through your self-degrading lifestyle that you deserve much better. What I am going to do today is show you that you are worthy of so much more. I promise you will get to know yourself today more than you thought possible, particularly in your final moments. With that thought I placed my two new friends in the box with Diana. I decided to call her Diana at this point as I would be spending several choice hours with her, getting to know her on a so much more profound level.

Copperheads are not aggressive snakes by nature but in a small space and with Diana perpetually squirming they would feel vulnerable enough to strike. They do not produce a fatal venom but a painful venom. I would let that pain be the lesson for the most part as I felt I should contact her body as little as possible.

Being in the bag must have made them provoked as they immediately inserted their fangs into her skin. One on the inner thigh and the other on her ample left breast. She screamed in terror. After two hours of her shrieking in pain and fear I realized I was basking in this more than the sexual favor she had granted me earlier. This was not what I had intended. I could take no delight from my teachings. This was not for me, it was for them. I was there to give back to my fellow human being.

"Are you enjoying this Diana?" I asked, shortly after her screaming had stopped.

"I... I can't... feel anything..." She responded. I noticed that she was no longer moving. The toxicant from the copperheads had paralyzed her. I was overwrought but felt maybe she had learned enough.

"Well... Do you feel like you have learned from this lesson? Do you feel alive?" I asked.

"Y-yes... Please..." She said, barely able to speak, obviously from excitement. She had really taken something from this.

"How do you feel Diana?"

"I... understand now." She responded.

"Is there anything you would like to say?" I asked.

"What?" She must have been thinking about this fantastic moment in her life because I knew she desired to thank me.

"Do you not want to thank me Diana? Do you not appreciate what I have done for you?" I asked.

"Yes... Thank... you." She said. I could not help but smile. I felt accomplished, like I had really done something great today. Then the proverbial other shoe dropped as she continued. "P-please let me go... I need... medical help... If you do... I will... please you... sexually... every... day."

I could not grasp what I was hearing. I thought she understood. I thought she had changed. Had I failed? Or was she not savable?

"I will... spread for you... any time... you want." She said. I could no longer take this. It was a figurative slap in the face.

"I am disappointed in you Miss Langley." I said, no longer calling her Diana as I realized I did not know her like I thought I would at this juncture.

In one swift motion and with more vexation than I care to acknowledge I grabbed my sharpest ax from the wall.

"No... Wait..." were her last words before I brought the ax down with a force nearly severing her head.

Diana Langley had not learned the lesson I had so nobly hoped she would but I had set her "Free" from a lifetime of having no fulfillment.

Chapter 4

Telly Rivers

Telly Rivers is quite different from anyone else I have ever had the pleasure of knowing. She belongs in this collection for the mere reason that she impacted my life in a very profound manner. Telly approached me one day as I was leaving my home.

"I know what you have been doing, you know." She said not in an accusatory manner but more of a curious statement as it seemed.

"Whatever do you mean young lady?" I responded.

"Cut the crap. I know you are taking people in your basement and killing them. "

I laughed. I knew it would not be convincing. I had never been much of a laugher. I never understood the purpose.

"I just want to know why." She elaborated slightly more. She was a spitfire to say the least. She was seventeen years old, had the mouth of a sailor and took guff from no one the least of all myself.

"Let's just entertain the thought for a second that you are right. What do you mean you want to know why?" I asked. I really was curious.

"You people always have some reason. You either want to rid the world of filth, you think you're getting some twisted form of revenge or you just plain get off on it sexually. So which is it?" She said even though one of these queries were correct.

"Popular culture jargon is all you are speaking." I replied.

"Fuck popular culture. I want to know why you do it." She continued.

"Quite a mouth on you young lady."

"Do you do it because you were picked on when you were a kid? Or did your mommy or daddy hit you a few too many times?" She asked. I really wanted to have a big laugh over this but I honestly did not know how.

"First of all, young miss, I was never picked on as a child and secondly my mother and father may have laid hands on me a time or two but I can assure you, I deserved it." I said and cast a gaze upon her that was meant to warn her off her questioning.

"Good. I'm glad you're not one of those pussies." She said and smiled for the first time. "So why do you do it?"

I stood there and thought about it for a second, not about why I do it but about the way I was feeling at the moment. I knew this girl was different. I could just deny what I had been doing but I had this strange feeling that it was right to admit it to her.

"What I do, I do not consider killing. I consider my work a service to the individual." I could not believe I was telling her this and most of all I could not believe the rush of excitement I was getting by telling her.

"Like how? What do you mean "a service"?" She looked as if she was concentrating on my every word.

"I teach them how to live through lessons in pain and then I set them "Free"."

"Bullshit! You don't set them free. I have been watching you. You carry them out of your house, sometimes in pieces, late at night." She spat her words at me.

"Young lady..."

"Call me Telly." She interrupted.

"Alright, Telly, lovely name, by the way." I said in a rather flattering manner.

"Please. My parents must have been on drugs when they gave me that name. Anyway... Continue please."

"When I say set them "Free", what I mean is I set them free from their meaningless existence and help them by allowing them to leave this world.

""Allowing them to leave this world?" Somebody's full of themselves." She said with irreverence.

"Maybe that was not the best choice of words on my part. What I am saying is I help them escape the oppressions of this world." I corrected myself. Telly really knew, even from the first time I met her, how to push my buttons.

"So you feel like you are having mercy on them?" She questioned.

"In a sense, yes but there is so much more to it than that." I stated.

"Good, I want you to teach me about your work." She said.

"My dear, you do not need to concern yourself with my work."

"Look, I'm not your dear. I'm not some innocent little teenybopper who is a fan of your work. I have been around the block in my seventeen years. The way I see it, you have two choices. Either teach me about your "work"..." She said with a minor eye roll. "Or I can tell the police what you have been doing and your ass will fry in the electric chair." I could not have loved this girl more if she were my own daughter.

"Do you think that is wise?" I asked with a deep gaze that left her unfaltering.

"I'm not afraid of you asshole. You can't hurt me more than I have been hurt before and killing me would do no good. I was dead the day I was born."

I relented. Over the next few months I taught Telly about my work. She was such a great student, learning so fast. She became a wonderful assistant. Her only flaw was getting a little too carried away when I allowed her to participate. She had inner anger and rage issues. I tried very hard to teach her to let the anger go but to no avail. Her anger, I would learn, stemmed from her drunken abusive father. Despite her condemning those who kill under these circumstances, she could not help herself. I felt for her.

I will speak more of Telly Rivers shortly but until that time is upon us I will speak of a man by the name of John Montgomery.

Chapter 5

John Montgomery

Telly had suggested John Montgomery to me as a possible candidate to be set "Free" before and even though I felt she presented a strong case, my pride would not allow me to let her choose someone to be taught a lesson. I gave in to her as I often did when she wanted something. Mr. Montgomery was a middle aged man who went from relationship to relationship never committing to anyone, he was an avid hunter for sport, which I absolutely detested and he was a bit of a con artist. He was collecting money from a local, very married, politician who he had caught in a house of ill repute that he himself frequented. Mr. Montgomery was a fine candidate indeed. I would teach him the error of his ways along with my assistant.

We took him as he was coming from the pawn shop that he owned up town. He was a fairly easy grab as he had been drinking for some time. We tied him to the table and retrieved a few tools including a hammer, some nails and his own hunting knife.

"Can we leave this one gagged? She asked.

"We cannot deny his ability to communicate through his pain Telly." I responded.

"I just don't want to hear his screams. It kind of freaked me out with the last guy. Next time I will be fine, I promise." She said. I gave in and gagged Mr. Montgomery.

Upon waking he looked shocked, they all do but there was something about his shock that seemed more intense.

"Good evening Mr. Montgomery." I said, trying to be comforting. His eyes were as wide as the moon. "My assistant and I have brought you here today to give you a lesson in living."

I have to admit, having him gagged was a great idea. I did not have to be subjected to their foul mouth and the horrible names they call me. I was able to concentrate on the task at hand.

Telly watched silently as I hammered the nails into his flesh. I felt as if Mr. Montgomery was understanding the lesson. This may have been because he couldn't speak but I really felt connected to his pain. After a couple hours Telly stopped me.

"Alright. That's enough." She said and I wondered at that moment if she was having second thoughts about this line of work. It really is not for everybody. "I want to finish him."

"Telly..."

"I have earned this. I have been learning from you for months. I want to set him "Free"." She said very convincingly.

"I do not know if you are ready." I said.

"I AM ready!" She said intently. "I have listened to every word you have told me. I have helped you torture people..." She said before I had to interrupt.

"Not torture Telly. We are helping them learn about living through pain." I said.

"Okay... Whatever." She responded.

"This is why I do not think you are ready."

"It was just a bad choice of words. I'm sorry. I am ready." She said.

Against my better judgment, I handed her the hunting knife. I could tell she was happy about this and that made me even more uneasy. I was correct to feel that way because I never expected what happened next.

She approached Mr. Montgomery and began speaking to him.

"I hope it was worth it you son of a bitch. I hope every time you put your hands all over me is going to haunt you in your last breath. Goodbye Uncle John!" She said with fire in her eyes.

"TELLY!!! NO!!!" I screamed but it was too late. She began plunging the knife into his chest repeatedly. I tried to pull her away but her adrenaline had turned her into something much stronger than I was. After what seemed like an eternity she finally backed down after making a terrible mess of this man and I set her on the bench.

"What did you do!?" I asked. I was not shocked by the gore in this situation but the brutality for which she attacked the man, who was apparently her uncle, was disturbing.

"What?" She said, still with a faraway look in her eyes.

"This was not what I have taught you."

"What's the difference? He's dead isn't he? "I could not understand why she would say such a thing.

"His being dead is not my purpose. Teaching him a lesson and setting him "Free" is my purpose." I said with as much anger as I could have for this young lady I had come to care about.

"You and your talk about this fucking "Free" shit. How about thinking about me for a second. Do you know what that bastard did to me for years?" She was crying for the first time since I had met her.

"What I do... What I was teaching you about is not about rage or anger. It is about doing something for someone else. It takes a certain discipline."

"I had to... I couldn't let him get away with what he did to me."
She said. I felt bad for her but I was still upset.

"Did you want to learn from me just for this?" I asked pointing at
the bloody man.

"You're my best friend." She said, looking up at me. "Hell, you're
my only friend. I have learned a lot from you but I have these things
inside of me. Things I can't control."

We agreed that she would no longer be my assistant but we would
still continue our friendship.

Chapter 6

Telly Rivers

Part 2

After that night I am happy to say that little changed in my friendship between myself and Telly. Well... not much until a few days before her eighteenth birthday.

"So what are you getting me for my birthday?" She asked as we were sitting in my living room watching some program about a group of whiny young adults from New Jersey.

"Your birthday?" I asked.

"Yeah, you know, that thing people have every year to celebrate their birth." She said, so smart beyond her years and too smart for her own good.

"What would you like?" I asked. Money really was no object and I would have bought her just about anything she wanted.

"What I want I'm not sure you will be willing to give me." She responded.

"You never know. Just ask me."

"I want you to teach me." She said and half smiled.

"Oh no... We tried that before and it did not..." I said before she stopped me.

"I don't mean in that way." She said.

"What do you mean?" I asked, though I already knew the answer.

"I want you to teach me a lesson in living and set me "Free"." There it was. My heart was beating so fast now I thought I was having a heart attack.

How could I do this? I cared very much for this young lady and the thought of harming her had never crossed my mind and was actually leaving me with a bad taste in my mouth. She tried her best over the next couple days to change my mind telling me she needed this. I went so far as to tell her that I would not see her on her birthday.

The night before her birthday she came over and it was almost like our previous conversations about setting her "Free" had never happened but as most things go with Telly, she could not drop the subject.

"You should fuck me before you set me "Free" tomorrow." She said rather bluntly. I spat my tea across the room after that statement.

"WHAT!?" Was all I could say.

"I'm just saying, we could have sex before you set me "Free"." She said. She was a very attractive girl with her long dirty blonde hair 5'5 inch stature and well developed body but that was not how I looked at her.

"Three problems with that." I said.

"And they are?" She asked.

"After my last sexual indiscretion I made myself so that I could never do anything sexually again and I do not think of you like that." I told her.

"Yeah, I don't think of you like that either. You're more like a young father that I wish I would have had. I just thought it would be nice to not "technically" be a virgin when I die... I mean I'm set "Free"." She replied. "Wait a minute... What's the third reason?"

"I am not going to teach you or set you "Free"."

"Why won't you at least think about it?" She asked.

"You are too young. You have not even had the opportunity to try to live without my lessons." I responded.

"From the day I was born all I have seen is violence. If my father wasn't beating me around my uncle was molesting me, my step-father doesn't give a shit about me and neither does my mother and I have only one friend, who is a serial killer..."

"I am not a serial killer!" I was offended.

"Say what you want but you're a fucking serial killer." She said. She knew how to hurt me. "My life is ruined. I will never be able to feel anything for anyone. My father disappeared on us a few years ago and I didn't care. I killed my uncle and have absolutely no regrets. I will never be able to have a normal relationship and God help any child I would possibly give birth to. Show me how to feel... I'm begging you."

"I cannot." I said.

"Why? For the love of God... Why?" She asked and I knew I had to tell her why.

"Because you wouldn't be here with me anymore." I blurted out.

"I will always still be with you." She said. "Is Julie not still with you?"

When she said that it brought everything to light. I knew I had to do this. It was not for me, it was for her. I would have to set my best friend "Free". She was not going to let this go. If I did not set her "Free" she would more than likely just kill herself in some demeaning manner.

She came over the next afternoon. I asked her one last time if this was what she really wanted. She told me it was what she wanted more than anything. She unclothed and I tied her to the table. She felt it was best to be tied down as she did not want to lose her nerve. I began going to work on her making my first cut at 6:02pm. She screamed. She screamed so loud I almost stopped but near the end I realized that I was doing a good thing for her. Before I set her "Free" I kissed her on the cheek.

"Thank you." She said, looking up at me. I knew she meant it. Unlike so many of the others, she was appreciative.

I made the final cut across her throat at 8:44pm. After she was gone I closed her eyes. I took her body to the little area behind the mall where she would easily be found. We never discussed it but I wanted her to have the dignity of a nice funeral. A few days later I learned through the local news that her last name was not Rivers. It was Spencer. She was the daughter of Doug Spencer.

Telly was right. The memory of her will always be with me. I feel her there alongside me every time I set someone "Free" and when I would leave my house I expected to see her standing there by my car as she often did. I never understood how to feel sorrow but not having Telly around was the closest I had come, even closer than when Julie had betrayed my love by laying with Telly's father.

Conclusion

The man stepped off the elevator and walked towards the secretary sitting behind the desk.

"Well hello Doctor." She said with a warm smile.

"Good Afternoon, Denise. You're looking lovely as usual." He said with a charming smile. "Is Mark available?"

"No. I'm afraid he didn't come in today." She said.

"Oh, has he taken ill?" The man asked.

"Apparently. He called in earlier and didn't sound too hot." She said. "You can go see Mr. Gamble. He'll take care of you."

"Thank you, my dear." He said before walking towards the door to Rod Gamble's office. He walked into the office and was met by a big almost weaselly smile from Rod, who was sitting behind the desk. He didn't enjoy dealing with Rod, who was very cocky and arrogant in his view.

"Another best seller?" Rod asked the man.

"Let's hope so." He replied.

"So what is this one about?" Rod asked.

"A deranged psychopath who thinks he is doing his victims a favor by torturing and killing them." He said. Rod laughed out loud.

"Continuing from your last two books I see. Sounds fantastic. I'm sure it will be a hit." He said. "So tell me something. How does an in demand surgeon, like yourself, have time to write these things." Rod asked pointing at the manuscript.

"You know me, Rod old boy. Always have to keep busy." The man said with a smile.

A few hours later the man started walking down the steps to his house thinking that he hoped his latest novel would go over well. He had written two other best sellers and hoped the trend would continue. He removed his jacket, placed his cane against the wall and walked over to the center of the room where a man was tied naked to a table.

"Have you lost your mind man?" The man on the table asked.

"Not at all Mark, old friend. You're going to be the subject of my next novel but don't worry, just like all the others I will change your name in my writings." The man said while reaching for his knife.

Dying Eyes

Melissa Joseph sat behind the cash register at her flower shop bored as she had been for the past 3 days. She had been running her flower shop, Blooming Business, for 3 years now. It was not a large flower shop by any means but Melissa's shop had done well the first two years of operation. Over the last year, though, business had gone downhill. The main reason for that was two new corporate backed flower shops opening in the city. Melissa noticed a decrease in business almost immediately. Even longtime friends who seemed like loyal customers had started going to the other flower shops.

"What am I going to do?" She thought to herself. She was beginning to realize that she would have to close her shop if sales did not improve soon. She had even taken two mortgages out on her house for business expenses. The thought of losing her home, which was left to her by her father, kept her up many nights. This had been her dream since she was a young child, planting and picking flowers in the backyard with her mother. Melissa's mother passed away when she was 14 and Melissa continued with the little backyard garden to this day. Now, at 35, facing a possible bankruptcy that would take her house and her business, Melissa felt like a failure.

It was 4:30 in the afternoon and she decided to close a little early. Normally the shop was open until 7:00 pm but considering she had only sold two dozen flowers in the past three days she didn't feel like sitting around waiting for nothing to happen.

On the way home she stopped by Dunkin Donuts where she purchased two blueberry cake donuts, her favorite when she was down. She drove slowly by the big flower shop in the city and cursed the owners under her breath.

"Patterson, South Carolina didn't need you." She mumbled as she drove away.

Later that night Melissa sat on her couch watching TV while eating the rocky road ice cream that served as her dinner.

"The only thing I am going to succeed in doing is getting fat." She said to her Persian cat Molly, who she was convinced was the love of her life. The closest Melissa had come to being a wife was an engagement that lasted 5 years, which ended in her catching her fiancé with his secretary in his office. Melissa had not so much as dated in 4 years.

The soothing sound of "Kashmir" by Led Zeppelin began playing from her cell phone, her favorite song since she was a child was her favorite ringtone as an adult. She was pleased to see the call was from her sister Amy. She loved her sister dearly, despite being slightly jealous that Amy had married a wealthy man and only had to work when she felt like it.

"Hello Love." She said excitedly when she answered the phone.

"Hello my Dear." Amy replied. It had been a tradition for years that they answered each other's call this way.

After a few minutes of catching up on each other's lives Amy asked the question Melissa was dreading.

"So, how are things going at your shop?"

"…Great." Melissa hesitated a moment with her response. She couldn't bear to tell Amy the truth. She knew if she was in trouble Amy would talk her husband in to giving Melissa money but she had too much pride, she couldn't accept money from her younger sister. She had always been Amy's protector growing up and wasn't about to lose that position.

"Are you sure? You didn't sound too confident there." Amy asked, genuinely worried about her big sister.

"Of course I'm sure silly butt. Everything is great. I'm even thinking of opening a second location." Melissa hated lying to her little sister but she didn't want Amy to worry about her.

"A second location?" Amy asked, surprised. "Weren't you close to losing the shop not all that long ago?"

"That was then, this is now little sis. Business is booming."

After her conversation with Amy, Melissa never felt so down on herself. Between lying to her sister and the tightness in her chest each time she thought about how nice it would be for business to be as good as she was trying to convince Amy that it was. "What am I going to do?" She thought to herself.

Once again Melissa had trouble sleeping. It was 3:00am and she needed to be at the flower shop by 7:00am. All she could do was think about the shop. She loved her shop and her house and couldn't bear to lose either. Molly laid next to her every night when Melissa couldn't sleep. It was like Molly knew Melissa needed the comforting.

"How did I get in to this mess Molly?" She said as she gently stroked the cat's very fuzzy body.

The startling sound of a knock on the door almost immediately brought Melissa to her feet. It was 3:00am and she couldn't imagine who could be at the door at this hour. Maybe it was her ex-fiancé at the door after all these years to beg for forgiveness. Considering that he showed no remorse for having sex with his secretary in the first place, she doubted this was the case but considered that it would be nice to slam the door in his face if it was him. She looked out the window to see a tall slender older man standing at her door soaking wet. It had been raining all night and the man, who looked to be in his seventies was soaking wet.

He looked harmless so she slowly opened the door.

"Can I help you?" She asked.

"No Melissa. I have come to help you." He said and stared at her like he was looking through her, making her feel very uncomfortable.

"I'm sorry?" She said, not certain if she had heard him right.

"I know your problems and I can see your solutions." He said. The stare continued. A shiver slipped down Melissa's spine. This man really creeped her out.

"Sir, if you don't mind I have to get up early…"

"Your flower shop is failing." He interrupted. "Soon you will be out of business. There are steps you can take. Unconventional steps that can make the future of your shop prosper."

"I'm not sure who you are or how you know I'm having problems with my shop but this really is none of your business." Melissa said.

"Try something Melissa; take Route 76 to work tomorrow instead of the highway. I will be back tomorrow night and you can tell me how your day went." He said in a very serious matter-of-fact tone. Something about the way he was speaking was almost making Melissa want to listen to him.

"Goodnight sir." She said before closing the door. She rubbed the chill from her arms. The man had walked away but she was still a little shaken from the conversation. She decided that if he came back tomorrow she was going to call the police.

The next morning, while having half a grapefruit, a piece of dry wheat toast and a cup of coffee, her penance for being bad the night before, she thought about the old man's stare.

"Who was that man and how did he know about my troubles with my shop?" She asked herself. She had never seen him in the flower shop or near it.

On her way to her flower shop while sitting at the red light she looked to her right and saw the sign for Route 76.

"I can't believe I'm actually considering this." She thought. "It will take me almost twice as long to get there." The inner urge she was feeling was too great. When the light turned green she turned right. Her trip on Route 76 was much smoother than she expected. There was nowhere near the traffic there usually is on the highway and she made it to the shop five minutes earlier than usual despite Route 76 being the long way around.

The day seemed no different. She had no sales and no customers stopped in. Other than her calm drive to work she would have said the old man was just plain crazy. That is until 3:00pm rolled around.

The phone rang. She was almost confused as she hadn't heard this sound in a while.

"Blooming Business. How can I help you?" She answered.

"I was wondering if you can help me. I am about to ask my girlfriend to marry me and I had this idea that I would like to cover her living room with flowers where I will pop the question. Money is no object." The man sounded very well educated and very excited about the proposal.

"Absolutely sir, I would be glad to help you." She said, every bit as excited as the man was.

On the way home she couldn't stop thinking about whether this was coincidence or whether the old man really knew something. "Impossible." She thought, though another part of her said otherwise. She decided she would hear the old man out if he showed up tonight at a decent hour.

She waited around until almost midnight. She was about to give up and go to bed when she heard a knock at the door.

"Good evening Melissa." He said as she opened the door.

She didn't wait to start into what she had to say. "So I took Route 76 this morning and sold more flowers this afternoon than I had in weeks combined. What is going on?"

"I see things Melissa." He stated. "It's a talent I have developed over the years."

"What do you mean "See things"?" She asked very confused but curious.

"I see things as they should be if things were done just a little different." He said.

"Like alternate realities?" She asked, even more confused.

"Something like that." He said, smiling for the first time. "My name is Ed Thompson. If you will let me I can help you."

"I'm still not sure I believe in all this but I basically have nothing to lose." She said.

"But everything to gain." He added.

"Why would you want to help me anyway?" She asked, very skeptically.

"Because you are in need." He replied.

"That doesn't really answer my…"

"We can squabble or I can tell you what the next step is." He interrupted.

"Ok." She said. "What's next?"

"What do you usually have for lunch?" He asked.

"Depends on my mood. I had tuna on wheat today and I was planning on a salad tomorrow." She answered.

"Have broccoli soup."

"Like cream of broccoli?" She asked. "Eww... I hate that stuff."

"Trust me Melissa and you will take Route 76 every morning now." Ed said. He seemed so confident and serious in his words that Melissa almost felt entranced.

"I like the Route 76 trip but I don't think I can eat broccoli soup every day."

"Just tomorrow." He said and laughed slightly.

"I will try." She said, hoping the soup would stay down.

"Goodnight Melissa." He said as he turned and started walking away before Melissa could say anything.

The next day Melissa gagged down a bowl of cream of broccoli soup. An hour later she had a customer and four customers and a phone order followed that. She felt terrible for being excited after she realized every sale was for a funeral. She always disliked selling flowers to mourners. She felt as if she was profiting from death. At this point, however, she was just happy to be making money. She had a long way to go to save her shop but things were looking up.

She was eagerly anticipating Ed's arrival tonight. She had much to talk about. She heard the door knock at a little after 10:00pm. He was getting earlier at least. She opened the door and before he could say anything and before she could even think about it she gave him a big hug.

"Well, good to see you too." He laughed.

"I sold so many flowers today Ed. I just can't believe it." She said with a smile.

"That is great and it is going to get even better." He said before his demeanor slightly changed. "Your next step is going to be a little different though."

"How different?" She asked, worried.

"Your neighbor reads your newspaper every morning before you get a chance to take it in." He said. "You know this because you have caught him."

"How do you know...?" She started to say before being interrupted.

"Because I have seen this happen over and over and so have you." Ed was getting more forceful with his words. This slightly intimidated Melissa, but also gave her a strange chill of excitement. "Yet you never say anything to him about it."

"I never say anything because I don't want to cause any trouble with my neighbors." She replied.

"Tomorrow morning you are going to say something." He stated with that creepy stare. "Oh lord it's back." She thought to herself.

"I don't know if I can do that."

"You must Melissa. This is the path to your successful future I am giving to you." He was almost yelling now. "You need to stand up to this man. Argue with him and tell him to get his own damn paper."

The next morning as soon as she woke up she looked out her window. Bob Simms was out there in his bathrobe, just like every morning, reading Melissa's paper. Perhaps it was Ed's words the night before, but she was really angry about it this morning. Usually she just found this an annoyance, but this morning it was like her blood was boiling from anger. She threw on a pair of sweat pants and a t-shirt, marched downstairs and thrust open the front door with a force so strong the wind from the door blew some loose papers off the desk next to the couch.

She walked up to Bob Simms. He was an older gentleman with a pot belly and a bad comb-over. He was not the world's most friendly neighbor and hardly ever exchanged pleasantries with Melissa unless she spoke first, and even then he was usually very gruff. He stood there and stared at her for a second not saying a word. His eyes glanced down and gave her body a once over. "Disgusting prick!" She thought to herself.

"What are you doing Bob?" She asked with a strength that surprised her.

"What does it look like I'm doing?" He asked sarcastically.

"It looks to me like you're reading my newspaper."

"Yeah. So?" He asked. Melissa was getting angrier by the second.

"So, it's my paper. I pay for it, I should be the first to read it." She retorted. "You are out here every morning reading my paper before I even get a chance to and you have never once asked."

"I don't know what your problem is lady…" Before he could finish she continued her rant.

"… and while I'm at it, I think Chompy is an adorable dog, but I'm sick of him shitting on the edge of my lawn. No more." She said and turned to walk away. She felt empowered, at least until Bob's next comment.

"What are you ragging or something lady?" He asked.

"You're such a pig." She said before going inside and closing the door. She stopped before she could move any further. She had remembered her conversation with Ed the night before. She swung open the door and yelled out. "Get your own damn paper!" She was very angry at this point.

That afternoon, after a very busy morning, she sat and reflected on her argument with her neighbor and couldn't believe that had actually been her. This was the first time in a long time where she actually felt like she could enjoy some down time. She leisurely watered some flowers in the back while listening to some calming music. She pondered what she was going to do next until she heard the bell ring signifying the shop door opening. She went to the front to see a goofy looking well-dressed man standing by the register.

"Can I help you?" She said with a smile.

"Good afternoon ma'am. My name is John Drake I'm a detective with the Patterson Police Department. I was wondering if I could ask you a few questions." He was all business. Melissa found this strangely attractive.

"Sure, what is this about?" She asked very confused. She couldn't imagine why a police detective would want to question her.

"Do you know the name Rodney Mills?" He asked. She knew the name immediately.

"Yes. He purchased several dozen flowers a few days ago." She replied.

"Mr. Mills apparently filled a young lady's living room with these flowers and strangled her when she came home to discover them." He said.

"Oh my God. He said he was proposing to his girlfriend." She said with her hand to her mouth in horror.

"From what we gather, the victim had never met Mr. Mills." He said. "Did you happen to meet Mr. Mills?"

"No. He told me to leave the flowers on the front porch because he was working late." She replied.

After several more questions the detective thanked Melissa for her time and smiled for the first time before leaving. As soon as the detective had left Melissa dropped to her knees. She felt horrible. She thought the man who had committed the murder seemed so sweet with his marriage proposal idea, but it was just a setting for death.

Her day only got worse when she got home. She found a large pile of dog feces on her walkway, obviously from her neighbor's five year old Irish Setter Chompy. She looked over at Bob Simms's house to see him standing in the window chuckling. "You asshole." She thought to herself as she glared at him.

That night when Ed returned she gave him a different kind of hug. It was more sorrowful as she began softly weeping.

"What's wrong Melissa?" He asked.

"Oh Ed..." She said through her tears. "... it's so awful. All I'm doing is profiting through death. Every sale I have had this week has been for a funeral, and today I found out I sold several dozen flowers to a killer."

"It's not your fault though, dear, you're just providing a service." He said very comfortingly. She almost felt better. "If you're not profiting off of these tragic events then the bigger flower businesses will. You're just trying to stay afloat at this point."

She felt a fatherly vibe from Ed. He knew what to say to calm her down. She had been upset all day but a few words from Ed set her straight. She had done nothing wrong. The connection she was feeling for Ed was very strong. He kind of reminded Melissa of her father.

"Are you ready for your next step?" He asked.

"Yes. I think so." She replied.

"There is a church just off Route 76 off Halleck Road." He said. She was a little worried. She hadn't been to a church in years. "St. Vincent's Catholic Church to be exact. I want you to stop there in the morning."

"Why?" She asked.

"Now listen to me Melissa this is important." He was being very curt but Melissa didn't mind. "I want you to go in to the confessional and confess to something. It doesn't matter what." She couldn't think of anything to confess to other than skipping school a few times as a teenager.

"I'm not Catholic though." She said.

"It doesn't matter. Confess to something, but before you leave say to the priest: "The Devil made me do it."." He said with a dead serious look.

The next morning Melissa was driving on Route 76. She had a huge knot in her stomach that was almost making her feel nauseous. She took Halleck Road, but when she got to St. Vincent's she froze. The confession was one thing but how could she say something like that to a man of God? The Devil made me do it? What was that supposed to mean anyway?

She finally found the courage and confessed to pre-marital sex. This embarrassed her, but she figured the man of the cloth had heard much worse. Before she could say what Ed had told her she froze. No matter how hard she tried she couldn't say the words.

"Is there something else I can do for you my child?" The priest asked after a minute or two of silence.

"No father. Thank you." She said before leaving.

"It will be ok." She thought to herself. "I did most of what Ed told me to do. It will be ok. Won't it?"

She had a very busy morning, but some down time around 11:00am. She decided to read her newspaper, which her neighbor hadn't touched that morning. She was stunned to immediately find an article about the girl that had been killed. She paused over the girl's name, Angela Dirkman. All of her orders this morning were for the Dirkman family.

"Oh Jesus." She thought. "I'm profiting even more off this tragedy."

By the afternoon, she had calmed down. She was still feeling really bad about the situation, but remembered Ed's words the night before about it not being her fault. A man walked in and immediately pulled out a badge and identification. He was as well dressed, but not as good looking as the man the day before.

"Hello ma'am, I'm detective Daniel Minnick from the Patterson P.D. Can I ask you a few questions concerning your order from Rodney Mills?" He asked. She was a little irritated. First of all she told them everything she knew and secondly, why couldn't they have sent the good looking detective from yesterday?

"I told the detective everything I knew yesterday." She proclaimed.

"I beg your pardon ma'am?" He said looking perplexed.

"The detective yesterday, John Drake, he asked me about Rodney Mills." She replied.

"Ma'am…" He said and paused for a moment. "Patterson P.D. didn't send anyone here yesterday and as a matter of fact there is no detective at the P.P.D. named John Drake." Her heart sunk. "Did he show you his badge?"

"No." Was all she could get out.

"Can you give me a description of this John Drake?" He asked, notepad and pen in hand.

"He was about six feet tall, very short hair and clean shaven."

"Any other distinguishing features?" Detective Minnick asked.

She thought about it for a few seconds and remembered something.

"I didn't see the entire thing but from under his jacket I noticed a tattoo of a spider on his wrist." She said.

"Ma'am…" He paused again. She wished he would stop doing that. "This sounds just like the description of Rodney Mills." He pulled out a sketch of Mills and Melissa immediately panicked.

"That's him." She cried.

Detective Minnick stayed for about an hour asking her more questions. He wasn't a very pleasant man and reeked of body odor and cigar smoke.

"Don't worry ma'am. We will get this guy." He said before leaving.

That night Melissa couldn't stop thinking about the day's events. She was, so much, looking forward to Ed's visit, but he never came. She waited until 6:00am until finally falling asleep on the couch. She woke up with Molly laying on her and a nostril full of fur. The feeling of dread hit her immediately.

She got dressed in a hurry and went to head out her front door. She hadn't had time for breakfast as she was already behind schedule. She stepped on to the porch without paying any attention. She felt her shoe sink into the squish. A pile of dog feces had been left on her porch. She knew who was behind this. She went upstairs and cleaned her shoe as she cried.

"Things were going way too good. Why are they falling apart now?" She asked herself. She couldn't help but think about Ed. Where was he last night? Had he given up on her?

She was on her way to work finally. After having problems getting her car started it seemed to be running well. She approached Route 76 and noticed flashing lights. Getting closer she saw that a semi was overturned and the entrance to the route was blocked.

"Wonderful!" She thought. "Can this morning get any worse? Can this week get any worse?"

The answer to that question was revealed to her as she came into town. She could smell the fire from a few blocks away and despite not being able to see it yet, she knew where it was coming from. She pulled up to see fire fighters working on the blaze but it was already too late. Her flower shop, all her flowers, her entire business was gone.

"I'm sorry sweetie. I would stay longer if I could, but Ben needs me back home." Amy said as she hugged Melissa. "He can't do anything for himself."

"It's ok. I understand." Melissa said though she didn't want to let go of her little sister.

Things had only gotten worse the last few weeks since the fire. The insurance company refused to pay on Melissa's claim saying the fire was "Under suspicious circumstances". They had heard Melissa was having financial difficulty and the fire had been ruled as arson. Though Melissa hadn't been suspected, the insurance company saw it differently. To make matters worse her neighbor, Bob Simms, had been telling the neighbors all sorts of lies about her, had taken to stealing her newspaper and was having Chompy, who was an innocent pawn in his twisted game, relieve himself on her lawn at least twice a day. To top it all off she hadn't seen Ed since the night he told her to go to St. Vincent's.

Later that night, she laid on the couch stroking Molly's fur. She was scared. She had no income, her shop was no more and the bank was already talking about taking her house. Amy and Ben both offered her money and/or a place to live but she was too prideful and couldn't accept.

The knock at the door startled her. She didn't even think that it could have been Ed, but there he stood. He looked at her almost in a shameful way.

"Where have you been? My world is ruined. I needed you." She said before he could speak.

"I'm sorry. Some things beyond my control happened." He said.

"I lost my flower shop. It burned to the ground."

"You ignored something I told you, didn't you?" He said in a fatherly tone.

"Yes and now I'm going to lose my house too…" She burst in to tears.

"Things can be fixed Melissa." He said looking into her eyes. "There is a way, but it is pretty drastic."

"I don't care." She continued crying. "I will do anything."

"Can I come in?" He asked. He had never actually been in her house.

"What do I have to do?" She asked as they sat on the couch.

"Brace yourself for this." He said, cryptically.

"Please." She said crying harder. "Whatever it is I will do it."

"You're going to have to take a life." He said and he looked so serious.

"What... I can't kill somebody."

"Think about it Melissa. Your success had everything to do with death. This is the only path I see that will return you to success. Taking a life will reset everything." He said.

"There has to be some other way."

"There is no other way." He said in a very cold manner.

"I can't do this... I'm not a killer." She said. She was very scared now.

"Can you live with losing your business and your house? Your future is very bleak at this point. In two to three years you will become very ill and the worst WILL happen. That is unless you reset the path." He said. He had been right all this time. How could he be wrong now?

"Who would I have to kill?" She couldn't believe she was even asking that question.

"Your next door neighbor." He said and then stared as she paused.

"Bob Simms?" She asked. She knew in her head that if she had to kill anybody it would be him.

"No dear." He replied. "… His wife."

"Ellen? She has never been anything but nice to me. She is the only neighbor that still talks to me after the things her bastard husband said." She said. Melissa was horrified.

"Think about it this way." He stated. "If you killed Bob, you would only hurt her but if you killed her it would hurt him."

Ed slept on her couch that night. She was awake all night thinking about taking Ellen Simms's life. She knew she had to do this to protect her own future, but how could she? She went downstairs to see Ed already up and petting Molly. She wished she hadn't let him stay. He was starting to scare her.

"You have to do this soon Melissa." He said first thing. She hung her head. "Bob has left for work. You need to get over there."

A half hour later Melissa found herself in the Simms's kitchen through the back door that had been left unlocked. Chompy, from behind a closed door just off the kitchen, began barking.

"Chompy, it's alright." Ellen Simms said as she came down the steps from the upstairs.

Melissa panicked and grabbed a knife from the kitchen and hid next to the refrigerator. It was such a clean and well-kept kitchen. It had such new looking and state of the art appliances.

"Must be nice." She mumbled.

"How am I going to do this?" She thought to herself. "She's a sweet lady, but this is for my future.

Melissa could hear Ellen slowly approaching. Her heart was beating so loud she was afraid Ellen would hear her. Ellen opened the refrigerator door and before Melissa could think twice she came from the side of the refrigerator and plunged the knife into Ellen's chest. The sound of the knife going into Ellen Simms made Melissa sick.

"Melissa…" Ellen said, laying on the floor, gasping for air. "Why?"

"I'm so sorry Ellen." Melissa wept. "I had to do it."

She ran out the back door and in her own back door. She was out of breath and to say she was distraught would be an understatement.

"Oh my God Ed. It was terrible." She said, hugging the old man.

"Did you do it?" He asked in a weird excited tone.

She looked at him for a minute and said. "Yes."

He started smiling and laughing. He jumped up and down like a kid who has just been told that school was cancelled for the day. She stared at him while she cried.

"How can you be so happy about this?" She asked. "I killed that poor innocent woman."

The day was a blur of flashing lights and police officers asking her questions. Seeing Bob sitting on his porch steps crying made her feel bad for him and very guilty. She was only able to sleep that night because of heavy medication.

She woke up and the clock next to the bed said 1:37pm. She knew she must go tell Ed he had to leave. She went downstairs to hear a knock at the door. A lady who looked to be in her late forties was at the door. Melissa opened the door and waited before saying:

"Can I help you?"

"I sure hope so." She said with a worried look. "I am going to every house in the neighborhood to see if anyone has seen…" The lady stopped in mid-sentence and looked over Melissa's shoulder. "There you are. I have been worried sick." Melissa turned to see Ed with a shocked look.

"I'm sorry… Daddy has been bad again." He said and burst into tears. Melissa felt sick. The lady turned to her.

"I'm so sorry. My father is an Alzheimer's patient and sometimes gets out of the house." She said to Melissa, who turned white. "He mostly gets out at night when the overnight caregiver falls asleep."

"Oh Jesus." Melissa said, though she meant to say it under her breath it came out very loud.

"I hope he wasn't any trouble. My name is Melissa Dane, by the way, I live down the street." The lady said.

Melissa couldn't speak now. She just closed the door and stood there. She watched as the lady walked off holding on to Ed's elbow. She was wondering why she couldn't have seen it before. Ed obviously wasn't normal but she refused to see it because she was in too deep with her shop. She just needed help. Maybe she was losing her mind too. At the moment it certainly felt like it.

"Oh dear God, what have I done?" She asked herself. "How did he know so much about my life? Had he been watching me?"

She was so distraught her body was trembling as she burst into tears. She almost didn't hear the footsteps coming up behind her over the sound of her own crying. She slowly turned and there he stood, Rodney Mills.

"Hello Melissa." He said.

Watching

I can honestly say that I never get tired of watching these kids. I sit here day in and day out watching them. Most days I wish they knew I was here but I'm afraid that would spoil the innocence of them playing as children do. Colleen, the little girl, is so beautiful with her light freckles and long flowing red hair and Johnny, her little brother with his sandy blonde hair and constant smile on his face. Come to think about it, they both have constant smiles.

Sometimes I think that they might know I'm here because they look towards my direction. They are still smiling but there is something different about the smile. Something I can't quite put my finger on.

Johnny loves to play with his little toy trucks, running them up and down the sidewalk pretending to be a truck driver. Colleen rides her little pink bike in circles out in the street all day long. If only I could have spent more time with them. I could have told them I loved them more, I could have been there to teach them right from wrong.

I wish I could just hug them and tell them everything will be okay but that's not possible. Everyone warned me that day but I didn't listen. I should have never gotten behind the wheel of that car. I should consider myself lucky that I can still see them but no one can be a good father to their kids when they are dead.

The Devil Walking Next To Me

I'm sure this is a dumb question but have you ever thought about what it would be like to be best friends with a serial killer? I'm sure you haven't and that's understandable. I, however, live with the guilt and irritations of being best friends with a serial killer every day of my life since I was 16 when my best friend, Tommy Jasper, committed his first murder. Before I get into all that let me introduce myself. My name is Joe Deen. Until a year ago I worked at a crappy little convenience store with my friend Tommy until we decided to buy the store and turn it into a comic book store, which was really our passion... Well... It was my main passion. Tommy's main passion was, obviously killing. So now I am part owner of a crappy little comic book store.

Tommy and I met when we were 13 and I was the subject of a bully taking out his aggression towards me for being smaller than him on my head. Tommy jumped in and beat the bully down. Now,

Tommy was no large kid and was much smaller than the bully but I could see those instincts in him that day which would lead to his first kill as he ruthlessly beat on this kid until he was a bloody mess.

Tommy and I spent the next few years hanging out, chasing girls and generally just being teenagers. Everything changed when we were 16. Tommy killed a weird guy from the neighborhood named Josh O'Dowell. O'Dowell had touched Tommy's little sister, Katie, in a suggestive way a few days before. Tommy was always protective of his little sister and still is to this day. For that reason alone I know that Tommy is not a total sociopath.

Tommy came across O'Dowell in the small park at the end of our street, where O'Dowell spent most of his days leering at the local children. Tommy bludgeoned him with a hammer. He came to my window that night and told me about it. At first, I thought he was joking but after a little while I could tell by the look in his eyes and his tone that he was dead serious. I was scared. Not just for what had been done but also for Tommy. *What would happen to him?* He had a moment of rage protecting his little sister. I couldn't let his life be ruined for this.

After that night Tommy was very quiet, hardly saying more than a few words when he came over and even fewer when we were walking to and from school. Eventually he stopped coming over and he wouldn't even look in my direction at school. I was devastated. Tommy had been my rock and the best friend I could have asked for until the night of his first murder. I felt like I had no one to talk to about school or girls or the girls at school.

After a few weeks Tommy showed up at my house. We went to my room and sat in silence for a few minutes. I finally broke the silence.

"What's going on man?" I said. Tommy said nothing. "Is this about what happened?"

Tommy sat with his head in the palm of his hands, sitting on the edge of my bed.

"It's alright Tommy, I didn't tell anybody and I'm not going to. You don't have to worry man." I told him.

"It's not that I'm worried about." He broke his silence.

"What is it? Tell me. You're my best friend. You can tell me anything." I said that and hoped he didn't think I sounded like a pussy.

"I liked it Joe... I liked it way too much." He said then he started crying.

"Killing that guy?" I said. I thought that was what he meant but I was hoping I was wrong.

"I..." He paused for a second. "Can still feel the hammer coming down on his head and it gives me chills of excitement."

"Oh shit Tommy." Was all I could say as he continued.

"I want to do it again so bad Joe.... It keeps me awake at night."

"Maybe you should talk to somebody." I said, trying to reassure him.

"Are you crazy? My old man would never go for that." He said. Tommy's father was a drunk at best and had knocked him around when he was younger. He had been raising Tommy and Katie since Tommy was six and Katie was three.

"Maybe if you talk to me about it... Maybe you could write down the things you want to do. It might help." And it did help for a few years. Despite Tommy desperately wanting to kill, he didn't for another three years.

He dealt with his aggressions in other manners. When Rob Nader, a school mate had made Tommy angry, he wanted to kill Rob so bad. I can't tell you how many times I had to talk him down. Instead of killing Rob he did something else to hurt him. He seduced and slept with Rob's mother, leaving so many clues that Rob found out. Unfortunately Rob's father also learned of the affair and was waiting for Tommy after school one day. He beat Tommy up pretty bad. Tommy told his father what had happened later. He knew it would be better to tell him the whole truth and deal with the consequences than for his father to learn the truth later. Instead of being angry with Tommy, he went to Rob Nader's house and assaulted the man who had beaten Tommy up and gave Rob a smack across the mouth on the way out.

"Nobody beats up my son and gets away with it." He would later say.

Tommy would continue the affair with Rob's mother for another year. His father didn't say a word when Tommy would bring her to their house. He told her when he turned eighteen he would take her away from the life she was living. Rob's father had other plans, as he moved them halfway across the country.

"Oh thank God." He said to me after he found out about the move. "I didn't want to be stuck with an old woman." Tommy never believed in love. Which, I'm sure, is because he is at least partially sociopathic.

Tommy's second victim had much to do with his sister as well. Like I said, he was very protective of his sister. If somebody messed with her they were in trouble. Don't even get me started on the incident surrounding Katie's first husband after Tommy found out He back handed her one day. Katie's high school science teacher, Derrick Sylvania or Mr. Sylvania as we had known him during our high school years, was a weaselly, stuffy prick. Tommy hated him, I didn't care for him much either.

Mr. Sylvania tried desperately to start a relationship, of sorts with Katie, who had grown into a very good looking young lady. Katie would have nothing to do with Sylvania, so he decided to harass Katie constantly during class. Causing her embarrassment every chance he could. He was also failing her despite her putting so much time and energy into her studies.

Tommy broke into Mr. Sylvania's house. He was coming out of his bathroom wearing a white wife-beater t-shirt and pink boxer shorts. Tommy said he wanted to laugh so badly but it would have defeated his purpose for being there. Tommy struck him over the head with the hammer several times before leaving Sylvania to bleed to death.

Now keep in mind, I never enjoyed Tommy's twisted tales of murder, I have never condoned or agreed with his way of life but he is my best friend. He has been there for me more than anyone else. He has told me that he has this feeling the second that he meets someone that he wants to kill. It's a compulsion. He can't let the feeling go until he kills them. I would like to say he only kills bad people but that is not the case. Most of the people do not deserve the fate Tommy thrusts upon them.

"I know you think I didn't kill anybody else after that weird guy in the neighborhood... wow... isn't that terrible... I can't even remember his name..." He said just the other day. I interrupted him because I did remember his name. I remembered all their names.

"Josh O'Dowell." I said.

"Yeah. Him. I killed somebody not long after him and before that fucking prick Sylvania." He said. I remember when he felt bad about his victims. Now he has become so flippant about them.

"Oh yeah." I said, giving him a stare.

"When I turned seventeen, my father called me down to the basement. He had a girl tied to a table. He handed me a knife and said 'today you become a man.' He left me in the basement with her. I knew my father was messed up but I didn't know he was a killer until that point. It was like he knew that I had the same instincts. I had killed Josh but, at least, I felt like I had a reason. I had no reason to kill this girl. I didn't even want to do it. I didn't have that feeling I usually get when I meet someone I want to kill but I didn't want to disappoint my old man." He said then looked away from me.

"What did you do Tommy?" I asked. I obviously knew what he had done and I didn't want details. I just wanted to know how he could kill someone that he didn't feel "that need" to kill.

"I just started stabbing her... I started plunging the knife into her. It didn't feel right. I don't know why my mind just clicks on certain people but others I would never even think about hurting... like you. Even if you decided you couldn't deal with it anymore and turned me in. I still wouldn't want to hurt you. Just like I would never hurt Katie."

"I don't like what you do, Tommy... but I promised you when we were sixteen and you told me about Josh, that I would keep your secret. I would really like to see you stop killing though." I said.

"I tried Joe... I can't... It's like a drug. If I meet someone I want to kill, I have to do it. It eats away inside me and before I know what I'm doing I am bludgeoning them with a hammer, stabbing them with a knife, burying an ax in their head..." He said before I stopped him.

"Okay Tommy, I get the point." I said before walking away.

A few days later I was running the register at the comic shop when she walked up. I never believed in love at first sight until this point. She just flowed as she walked towards me. She was tall, had long brown hair, brown eyes that shined in the dim light of the store, and a smile that made me want to drop to my knees and beg for her hand in marriage. I hadn't even said a word to this girl yet but I was already head over heels.

"Spider-man fan are ya?" I said. Oh God such a dork. Couldn't I have come up with something better?

She laughed and said "Oh yeah. I have loved Spider-man since I was a little girl."

"He's one of my favorites too." Pull it together Joe, you're losing it.

"How long have you worked here?" She asked. A question... she asked me a question. That has to be a good sign. I struggled to get out my reply.

"I actually own the place with my buddy Tommy." I said. Okay genius add to the story... Talk already.

"That's so cool. I love comics." She said. "I think guys that work in comic book stores are hot" Yep. I just swallowed my gum. I couldn't speak because she would know that I was choking. I took a big drink of the coke that had been siting for six hours next to the cash register.

"That's very interesting." I said with such eloquence. She was smiling at me. I didn't know what to say. I'm not so good with girls.

"Do you like video games and beer?" She asked ""Cause they are my other two favorite things."

"How is it that your three favorite things are my three favorite things?" I asked, smiling.

"I don't know but I think we should enjoy them together sometime." She said. Was this really happening? Did the girl of my dreams just ask me out? My name's Sherri by the way."

"I'm Joe. Very nice to meet you Sherri."

I took down her number and watched her walk away. To most she would seem very plain looking but to me she was a goddess and she was like me but with boobs.

Tommy walked over to me passing her on her way out.

"Oh man." He said to me.

"I know." I said, thinking that he found her attractive as well. I couldn't wait to tell him that I had a date with her but before I could, he said something that turned my stomach upside down.

"That girl... I had the feeling when I saw her. I need to kill her." He said. I was floored.

"What? No... Tommy."

"Yeah. I felt it the second I saw her. I'm already having visions of putting a knife into her." He said.

"Tommy. I made a date with her. She's like the girl I have waited my whole life to meet." I said, hoping to change his mind.

"Don't be crazy Joe. She's just another girl there's a lot of them out there." He said. What he failed to realize is that I'm 27 and have never been on a date with a girl. Which, yes, means I am a virgin. I'm overweight, I have shaggy long curly hair, a long beard and I wear glasses. No girl should ever want to date me but here is this perfect girl who asks me out. I vowed that Tommy was not going to get his way this time.

I hadn't seen Tommy in hours. He hadn't helped close the store at all. This was unlike him. He usually feels like he has to stand over me no matter what I do. I had to find him and talk him out of this.

I walked in the back and wished I hadn't found him. He was picking up the rubber sheets and cleaning up the bloody mess he had made. I had a sick feeling in my stomach that he had already gotten to Sherri.

"Oh my God Tommy! You told me you wouldn't do this at the store anymore." I said.

"I'm sorry man. I just got the urge and couldn't control it." He said with a huge smile. Killing did make him happy.

"This wasn't the girl from this afternoon was it?" I asked and prepared myself for the answer.

"In a sense." He replied. *In a sense?* What the fuck was that supposed to mean.

"What are you saying Tommy? Was this the girl or not?" I said, getting angrier. I just knew he had gotten what he wanted again.

"Not physically but mentally. I was so inspired by the feeling I got from seeing the girl and that energy that I had to find someone to kill."

"What happened to the months of research and working through your plans for your kills? This is getting out of control Tommy." I said. I had gone as far as to cover for Tommy in the past by giving him an alibi. My conscience, actually, physically hurts most of the time. I have never had the desire to kill anybody but my not turning Tommy into the police was enabling him. He was my best friend though, probably my only friend.

"It was an impulse. How many times have you been at the cash register at a grocery store and grabbed a Snickers at the last second?" He replied. What kind of logic was this?

"That's not the same Tommy?" I said.

"Why isn't it?" He asked.

"Because I'm not killing anybody with the Snickers." I said. He was really irritating me.

"You're killing yourself. I've been meaning to talk to you about this. I'm a little worried about you." He said.

"Are you serious?" I asked.

"What?"

"You kill people Tommy!" I said. This had to be the angriest I had ever been with him. "How can you compare that to me eating a Snickers? You know what! Just forget about it... Tell me this much at least. Now that you killed... Whoever this was... Are you still going to kill Sherri?"

"Sherri? Oh man, that helps me so much. Thanks for getting her name buddy." He said. Why? Why did I mention her name? That was so dumb.

"I didn't get her name for that reason. I told you I have a date with her. You cannot kill this one Tommy!" I said.

"I have said this a million times Joe. I can't control myself when I get the sign. I'll tell you what I will do for you though. I'll wait until you fuck her first." He said.

"This isn't about fucking her Tommy. I fell in love with her the second I saw her."

"What a bunch of crap!" He replied. "It doesn't work that way man."

"Just because you can't love doesn't mean no one else can." I said. That would have been a harsh statement if I wasn't talking to a cold blooded killer.

"That's not true. I love my sister... I love you like a brother." He said. Okay, I know he's a serial killer but it was nice to hear that.

"I love you too man but if you did, indeed, love me like a brother, you would leave this girl alone. Give me a chance to be happy." I said and I meant it. I really did love him like a brother despite hating his habits.

"Oh... Alright..." He said and I felt on top of the world. "For you I will let this one go but it's going to be hard. She just looks so... so... killable. I have to go... I need to find someone else to kill." It was so wrong that I was okay with that. Someone else was going to die but the girl I was going to marry and have kids with, at least I hoped, was going to live.

Sherri and I began dating. She was everything I hoped she would be and more. Tommy seemed to be handling it well. He did pause for a moment with the knife he was using to cut the roast with, the time that the three of us had dinner together. It was hard sometimes lying to her when she would ask where he was going when he would leave late at night. I told her that he was a raging alcoholic and that seemed to satisfy her curiosities. Finally after a few months Tommy came to me in frustration.

"I can't do this. I need to kill her Joe." He said.

"You promised you wouldn't!" I reminded him.

"Come on, she's not even that great." He said.

"What do you mean?"

"I see the way she controls you." He was grasping at straws now. "Always like 'do this, do that'. She's very controlling."

"She is not!" I said, not believing what I was hearing. "Name one time she ever tried to control me!"

"The other day... She was like 'Hey Joe, I need you to do this.' and you were like 'Sure I"ll get right on that.'..." He paused for a second, not sure where he was going with this. "... God dammit Joe! I need this!"

"It's not going to happen Tommy." I said, as he ran his hands through his long hair in frustration. "In fact... Maybe you should find someplace else to live."

Tommy and I had been roommates for three years. He was a perfect roommate. He was clean, neat, never loud and a great cook, even though I had my initial worries after I found the book about Jeffrey Dahmer but we talked through that. It was sad to see him packing his things.

"What's going on?" Sherri asked. She came over as Tommy was leaving to take his stuff to his new place. An apartment he had found for really cheap just uptown.

"Tommy's moving out." I said and was surprised to see her acting very upset about it.

"Fuck... This is going to ruin everything." She said, stomping her feet in anger.

"No sweetie." I said, not quite sure why she was upset. "This will be the best thing for us. I need to tell you something."

"What is it Joe?" She said in a sarcastic tone. I wasn't sure why she was changing her attitude all of a sudden.

"I love you." It felt good to say those words to her. To finally express how I had felt since the first time I saw her. Her reaction was nowhere near what I had expected. I thought she would put her hands to her mouth and make that 'Awwww' sound that women make in movies when a man says something sweet to them. Maybe a few tears would have even been nice. What I got was:

"Yeah I don't think so." She said as she reached for the Superman lamp that was sitting on the table behind the couch.

I woke up tied to a chair. I don't know if this was more hurtful or if seeing my Superman lamp on the floor in a million pieces bothered me more.

"I'm sorry I had to do this... No... Actually I'm not but I'm doing it anyway." She said standing over me with a huge knife.

"Please tell me you were only slicing bread with that knife." I said. I knew it wouldn't break the tension but I had to keep myself sane.

"No, dear." She replied. "I'm going to kill your friend Tommy with this knife then I'm going to kill you with it.

"Why? I don't understand." I really didn't.

"Tommy, that fuck, killed my brother Josh when I was just a little girl." She said.

"Josh O'Dowell?" I asked.

"So you knew about it too? I really don't feel bad now. Not that I did before." She said very coldly.

"I didn't help him or anything."

"You knew and said nothing. You're just as guilty." She said, stopping to take a deep breath before continuing. "I have been waiting for so many years for this. I started watching you and knew the perfect way to get to Tommy was to get close to you first and it was so easy. You just fell right into my plans. Then you had to ruin it with your little lover's quarrel."

"So you used me." I said, hurt.

"How could you think I would fall for a loser like you?" She said. That really hurt.

I heard Tommy's car pulling up. She ran to the window and got a huge smile on her face. I still loved that smile despite the turn our relationship had just taken. She shoved a sock in my mouth that I hoped was clean and put duct tape over my mouth.

Tommy walked in to see me tied to the chair. Sherri was hiding behind the door, of course. His first reaction was:

"Oh God. I didn't mean to interrupt. I'll get my things and you two can finish your little game. He wasn't very bright sometimes. Sherri let out a loud grunt, which Tommy apparently heard, and started running towards him with the knife. Tommy turned around and caught her arm. He flipped her and she landed back first on the floor where she immediately spun around and tried to stab him in the leg. Tommy had excellent reflexes and jumped to avoid the knife.

"What the fuck is going on?" He asked as she was getting up.

"You killed my brother now I'm going to kill you genius." She said, hissing.

"You'll have to be a little more specific. I kill a lot of people." He said.

She ran at him with the knife again. He brought an open hand down on her wrist sending the knife flying to the floor. She punched him in the face sending him over the couch. I know it was wrong that the force of her punch turned me on but I had always had a thing for Wonder Woman and at that moment she reminded me of Wonder Woman, a psychotic and deranged Wonder Woman but Wonder Woman none the less.

Tommy stood up and tackled her the second she came around the front of the couch. He held her down.

"Crazy bitch!" He grunted, trying to catch his breath.

"I'm going to kill you, you bastard." She replied. Then it came. They kissed. I wasn't offended. One, because I had pretty much accepted that our relationship was over and two, because Tommy had told me before that he had feelings of sexual tension often when he was struggling with a female victim.

The kiss ended with Sherri's knee to Tommy's groin. He rolled away as she ran to pick up the knife from the floor. She jumped on him and stabbed him in the shoulder. She had been aiming for his chest but Tommy partially deflected the knife. She pulled the knife out and went straight for his chest. Tommy grabbed her hands that were firmly wrapped around the knife. Tommy was no weak man but he was struggling to keep the knife from going into him. Sherri had obviously prepared for this moment.

Tommy took one hand off the knife and connected on her jaw with a wild punch sending her to the floor. As Tommy was standing up, Sherri charged at him, apparently not seeing the knife, which she had dropped, in his hands. She ran stomach first into the knife and crumpled to the ground.

"Oh... you … bastard." She said as she struggled to take her last few breaths.

"Are you okay buddy?" Tommy asked as he was untying me.

"Yeah." I said, trying to catch my breath.

"What was that?" He asked, looking down at her lifeless body.

"Josh O'Dowell's little sister." I replied.

"I didn't even know that perv had a sister." He said, wincing in pain from his wound.

"She basically used me to get to you."

"That's crazy." He said, pausing for a second. "At least you're not a virgin anymore."

I looked down at her and felt very sad. I had loved this girl. I wanted to marry this girl and have kids with her and now she was dead. She was crazy but who was I to judge? After all my best friend is a serial killer.

Trick or Treat

Milton Burke sat in the dark room, the same as he did every year on Halloween. Milton had been home bound for a few years. He had an overwhelming social anxiety that prevented him from making friends and having any kind of social activity. He had been paying a neighbor to go to the grocery store for him every two weeks but lately his anxiety had gotten so bad that he would have the neighbor, a teenage boy named Donnie, leave the groceries on his porch and he would retrieve them after dark when he felt safer to open his door.

Despite his condition, Milton loved Halloween. Every year he would have a big bowl of candy to hand out to the children who were trick or treating in the neighborhood. The only problem is, he had been doing this for the past 12 years but he had never had anyone come to his door. This, in part, was because Milton didn't realize he should have his porch light on and also the fact that the children in the neighborhood were afraid to go to Milton's door.

Since Milton never left his home there were many tales about the strange man in the dark house.

Milton had chosen to dress up as a ghost this year. *How appropriate*. He thought to himself. *I might as well be a ghost.* Last year he was dressed as a clown and the year before he had been dressed as a wizard. Milton knew it was irrational but over the past few years he had started to grow angry and bitter over the children not coming to his door on Halloween night. It angered him mostly because it was the one day out of the year where his anxieties didn't affect him as usual. He felt safe in his costume and almost human.

15 years later.

The man, tied to the chair, looked up at the stranger dressed up as a pirate, complete with a patch and a fake parrot on his shoulder.

"Please... Just let me go I have a family." The man in the chair said.

"I'm not letting you go. You owe me." The pirate said.

"What... What do you mean?" The man asked.

"Every year I would dress up and be ready to hand out candy but you and your friends would never stop at my house." The pirate replied.

"What the hell are you talking about?"

"I have been sick for a long time. Halloween is the one day of the year I felt good about myself but no one ever wants to trick or treat at my house. I'm giving you the opportunity now. I'll give you a choice." He said as he pulled a large bowl of candy from a cabinet. "Now decide. Do you want a trick or a treat?"

"What?" The man said.

"It's simple. Do you want a trick or a treat?" The pirate asked.

"This is crazy..." The man said.

"DO YOU WANT A TRICK OR A TREAT?" The man dressed as a pirate yelled, angered that the man wasn't cooperating.

"You need help." The man said.

"Fine. I will decide for you. You get a trick." The pirate said as he reached for the sword attached to the sheath on his hip. One flick of the pirate's wrist was enough to completely sever the man's head.

"Milton Burke wishes you a Happy Halloween." He said to the, now decapitated, man.

Milton stepped back and smiled. This was the fifth year Milton had been having his "Halloween Party". He always dressed up nice for them, usually three or four people. He would take them into the kitchen and offer them the choice between a trick and a treat. He had four guests this year and had just finished with the first guest.

Milton retrieved an older man, who he had dressed as Robin Hood, from the living room. He pulled the chair he was tied to through to the kitchen while the man grumbled through his gag. He took the gag off and immediately regretted it.

"WHAT THE HELL ARE YOU DOING YOU LITTLE FREAK?!" The man yelled at Milton. "You fucking little shit! I'll kick your ass as soon as I am out of this chair."

"Is that any way to talk to the host of your party?" Milton asked him.

"Party? You call this a party?"

"Yes sir this is the neighborhood Halloween Party. You are privileged to be only one of four invited." Milton said.

"What is wrong with you?" The man asked. "What is the meaning of this?"

"This is your penance for never coming to my house for trick or treating." Milton said.

"Are you crazy? I must be a good twenty years older than you. I would've been too damn old to
Trick or treat by the time you were born." He proclaimed.

"I think you're mistaken." Milton said, smiling through his fake beard.

"Listen... Why don't you just let me go and we'll forget all about this. I won't even say anything about the guy and the dame in there."

He said, gesturing his head towards the living room.

"All I want you to do is choose. Do you want a trick or a treat?" Milton asked, not taking his eyes off the man.

"That's it? What a fucking little freak." The man mumbled.

"Just pick a trick or a treat and we're done here." Milton said as he placed the bowl of candy in front of the man.

"No... I'm a really bad diabetic. One piece of that shit'll kill me. Just give me one of your fucking tricks. Whattaya got? A water balloon or somethin'?" The man scoffed. Milton couldn't wait any longer. He was tired of the old man.

"A water balloon?" Milton said with a giggle. "Nothing quite so childish." He said as he pulled out his pirate's sword.

"Oh you're gonna use your little kiddie sword huh?" The man said smirking. Milton brought the sword down across the man's neck. He couldn't listen to him any longer.

"Did it feel like a kiddie sword?" Milton said to the lifeless man in the chair.

He took a few minutes to reflect before getting the man dressed as a vampire from the living room. He stopped to think of some of the parties he had thrown over the years. He remembered the man he dressed like a pig and then slaughtered him. The man dressed as an outlaw that he defeated in a gunfight using a knife. Milton was happy the entire year ever since he started having his Halloween Parties.

When he took the vampire man's gag off, he was already sobbing.

"P-please don't hurt me." He said to Milton.

"Shouldn't a vampire be braver?" Milton asked.

"I'm... I'm not a vampire."

"You are tonight and I will exact my revenge on you." Milton said.

"Why? What did I do?" The man asked sobbing a little more.

"You didn't drink my blood like a typical vampire would but you did break my heart." Milton stated.

"How?" The man dressed as a vampire asked.

"Now you have two choices. Trick or treat?" Milton said, ignoring the man's question.

"I'm sorry if I broke your heart?" The man said softly.

"Trick or treat?" Milton asked.

"I didn't realize I had hurt you so bad." The man continued.

"Trick or Treat?"

"Is there anything I can do to make it up to you?" He asked.

"TRICK OR TREAT?!" Milton yelled. He took out his sword and without hesitation cut the man's index finger on his left hand off.

"TREAT... TREAT... FOR GOD'S SAKE, TREAT!" The man yelled out in pain and horror.

"Excellent. A treat for me." Milton said. He pulled the man's head back by his hair and smacked the blade of the sword against his throat, cutting his windpipe and severing his carotid artery. "I just don't like vampires. They're too scary."

He felt accomplished. He felt like he was somehow improving this evil world that shunned him and forced him to have such fear that caused him to not leave his house except for one day out of the year.

Milton dragged the chair with a lady dressed as an angel tied to it. She was already panicking. *Not another one who won't choose.* He thought to himself. He hated when they wouldn't decide. It was just as hurtful as them not stopping for candy.

He looked at the lady before going to the living room to peak out the window. He had heard some children and thought they might actually stop at his house. He had never given up hope even after 27 years without a single trick or treat-er.

He sighed as the children passed by without stopping. "Oh well... When they become adults, I won't give them the choice. They will have to come to my house for trick or treat time."

He walked into the kitchen and slowly removed the gag from the angel lady. Of his four guests this lady is the only one whose name he knew. Her name was Karen and he only knew that because she had lived next door to him since she was a child and had heard her mother yelling her name on occasion. He thought she was so sweet and cute as a child, he did love children, but she was not a child any longer and the fact remained that she never stopped at his house for trick or treating.

"Why are you doing this?" She asked.

"It's Halloween. You're an invited guest at my party. Now you get the chance to decide." Milton said.

"Decide what?"

"Do you want a trick or a treat?" He asked.

"P-please d-don't hurt me." Karen said.

"You hurt me every year. You never stopped for candy. I dress up every year for the kids but no one ever stops to trick or treat at my house." He said.

"I'm sorry..." She said, sobbing. She knew exactly where she was. She could see her house through the crack of the curtains in the kitchen. "I was scared. My mom always told me to stay away from your house and it was always so dark."

"You can make it up to me now by telling me your choice. Do you want a trick or a treat?" He asked.

"So I get candy if I choose treat but what do I get if I choose trick?" She asked.

"I can't tell you that. It's a surprise." He said with a wicked smile.

"I choose treat." She said. The man before her had chosen treat as well but he wasn't going to change her decision. "Maybe she deserved a treat." He thought to himself.

He took the candy from the cabinet. He unwrapped a piece of the chocolate candy and held it out to her. She took it in her mouth, chewed it and swallowed.

"Thank you." She said, happy that she would get out of this alive. "Can you let me...?" She stopped in mid-sentence and started choking. Her mouth became really dry and her throat was burning.

She tried to regurgitate but couldn't. After about a minute of struggling she gave in to the poisoned candy and slumped down in the chair.

"Ahhh... Such a great party. I hate to see it end. I hope you all had a good time." He said, looking at the four bodies on the kitchen floor. "Time to clean up, I guess."

As he was about to go to the basement to get his electric knife, he was startled by the doorbell. He shut the kitchen door and slowly walked to the front door. He couldn't imagine who it could be. He opened the door to see a little girl dressed as a fairy princess.

"Trick or treat!" The little girl said. Milton almost didn't know what to say.

"What a lovely little princess." Milton said, grabbing the bowl of the un-poisoned candy and dropping a handful into her bucket.

"Thank you mister." She said with a smile.

"Well you are welcome little lady." Milton replied. The little girl turned around and yelled out to some kids who were about to walk past.

"Over here guys." She said to them. "He's really nice."

Three boys, one dressed as a ninja turtle, one dressed as a cowboy and one dressed as a fire fighter, came over to Milton's porch. He filled their buckets as well as the little girl's bucket with candy.

"Thank you sir." The cowboy said.

"You're welcome young man." Milton said.

"Cool sword... Awesome... You even have fake blood on it." The fire fighter said to Milton. He looked down at the sword and shrugged his shoulders.

"I knew the other kids in the neighborhood were stupid." The ninja turtle said. "I told them I thought you would be a nice guy. Thanks for the candy."

Milton slowly closed the door as the children ran away. He couldn't stop smiling. He was happier than he had ever been. *Why couldn't they have stopped by for trick or treating five years ago? I wouldn't have had to throw my parties.* He thought to himself.

He walked towards the center of the living room, still smiling. Suddenly he stopped dead in his tracks. He clutched his chest as the tightness and pain immobilized him. Before he knew what was happening he crumpled to the floor, lifeless.

Rosie

He walked up to the very old looking farmhouse all the while thinking and wondering "How did I get here?" The question didn't really pertain to the farmhouse it was really a question of how he had gotten to this point in life. Jeff Travis had grown up a fortunate son. His father a well-known heart surgeon and his mother a political activist for woman's rights. Jeff had always been one to rebel against his parents not wanting or taking any financial help that they would offer him. Instead Jeff chose to make his own way in life. At this point, though, Jeff was wondering if he had made the right decisions for himself seeing that his 1984 Ford Fairmont broke down in the middle of nowhere, leading him here to this farmhouse in the very small town of Outcrop.

Jeff knocked on the door and worried slightly. He had seen way too many horror movies that began this way. He couldn't imagine what the person who answered the door was going to look like or be like.

"Well hello stranger." The lady said. She looked nothing like what Jeff had feared. She was maybe in her late thirties or early forties with long dark hair and blue eyes. She was not a stunningly beautiful woman but was not hideous in the least bit.

"Hello." He struggled to get out. "I hate to bother you but my car broke down about a mile up the road. My cell gets no reception out here. Is there any chance I could make a call to get a tow truck or something?

In fact, Jeff's first call was going to be to his mother. He had not a penny to his name at the moment. Jeff had always been closer to his father and always felt as if his mother resented him for not being a girl. Unfortunately, after the last fight he had with his father, concerning his father feeling Jeff should get his act together, he didn't feel comfortable asking him for money.

"Of course you can." She said with a smile. "Come on in. The phone is right here. I haven't had a cell phone since moving here 15 years ago. There is absolutely no reception in this neck of the woods."

"Thank you so much. I will be quick. I promise," He said, returning her warm smile.

He dialed his mother's number but only received a message that said the number was no longer in service. *Did my mother really change her number without telling me?* He thought to himself.

Just as Jeff hung the phone up a rather large, young looking man walked in dressed in overalls and a long sleeved flannel shirt. Despite his size he looked about as threatening as a teddy bear. He had an athletic build and looked to be not far out of high school.

"What's going on here honey? Are you cheating on me again?" He looked very serious and straight forward when he said this. Jeff felt a lump in his throat for a minute, wondering if the young man's non-threatening look was deceiving. The young man looked back and forth to the lady and Jeff a few times before busting into a laugh. "How are you doing? My name is Todd Matthews. This is my wife Ellen Matthews." He extended his hand and gave Jeff a hearty handshake.

"Where are my manners?" Ellen said, looking embarrassed. "I never even thought to introduce myself."

"That's okay. I should have done the same. My name is Jeff Travis." Jeff said to Ellen before turning his attention back to her hulking husband. "My car broke down about a mile up the road. Your wife was nice enough to let me use the phone."

"I saw a car while I was in the field. A green Ford Fairmont?" Todd asked.

"Yes that's my pile of junk." Jeff said, hanging his head.

"You're welcomed to wait here until whoever you called comes." Todd said, not realizing that Jeff had not gotten through to his mother.

"Only problem is I called my mother and, apparently, she has changed her number without telling me. I'm ashamed to say I have no money. Is there a town not far up the road where I was heading?"

"Not for miles. At least twenty." Ellen said.

"We don't really have any money to spare or we would help you out, but if you would like you can stay here for the night and we can go up in the morning to take a look at your car." Todd said with a welcoming smile.

"I don't want to impose on you. Really, a walk would do me good." Jeff stumbled to say.

"Nonsense." Ellen exclaimed. "We insist. Besides it will be dark soon and when it gets dark around here it really gets dark."

"Thank you very much. I consider myself very lucky to have come to your door. I have seen way too many movies." Jeff laughed which brought laughter to the Matthews'.

"You can go upstairs to clean up, Todd will show you to your room and then we can have dinner at eight. How does pork chops, mashed potatoes and gravy, green beans and biscuits sound?" Ellen asked

"Like I have died and gone to heaven... Have I?" Jeff asked jokingly, which caused some laughter.

"After eating my wife's cooking you'll wish you had." Todd said with a laugh before being playfully slapped on the arm by his wife. What followed was a quick make out session between the two that made Jeff feel very uncomfortable but he didn't care. He somehow felt like he knew the Matthews, like he was just visiting some old friends.

"This is delicious." Jeff said as he downed his third pork chop and finished his second helping of mashed potatoes and gravy.

"Do you never eat, Jeff?" Ellen asked.

"Yes but usually spaghetti out of the can or McDonald's when I'm lucky." He said while chewing. His mother would not be happy with him for that. *Never talk with your mouth full.* She would always say.

"Do you mind me asking what you do?" Ellen asked.

"I work at a video rental store."

"A dying breed." Todd exclaimed. "Everything is digital anymore. DVDs will be a thing of the past soon."

"Yes. We don't get a lot of business and it doesn't pay well but I am happy with my job. I get to interact with people and I get to watch a lot of movies." Jeff said   smiling. Jeff really did enjoy his job and his life as a matter of fact. He lived the simple life. He went to work came back to his apartment, played video games and watched movies, drank as much beer as he wanted and didn't have a girlfriend to nag him not to. That was what his parents were for.

"Well I'm glad you're happy with your job Jeff. I really enjoy mine too. I take care of the farm."

"…And he does a very good job of it." Ellen interrupted. "I am a school teacher in the neighboring town of Raven Valley…"

"That's how we met." Todd also interrupted; the statement caused a glare from Ellen which seemed to be because she wasn't ready to have that conversation. "I was one of her students in the fourth grade. I ran into her two years ago at church and the rest is history."

"I didn't remember Todd as one of my former students when we first met and I felt very strange about dating someone I had taught when they were a child but we had such a connection that I couldn't keep myself away from him." Ellen exclaimed as she stared at Todd. "That and he's hot." They all laughed again.

"I think that's great." Jeff said. "Love is a beautiful thing. Not everyone gets to experience it." The truth was that Jeff didn't really care about love. He was very much a loner. He enjoyed talking to others and having friends but women just complicated his life. He didn't like the way they always tried to make him achieve more than he wanted.

After a nice conversation with the Matthews about religion, movies and movies based on religion Jeff asked if it would be okay if he went to lay down. He was very tired. Walking a mile in the sun had taken a lot out of him.

Despite being tired Jeff tossed and turned. He heard a banging sound that wasn't helping him stay asleep either. Jeff was no stranger to sleepless nights. He had more than he cared to have. This was different, though, he was exhausted but still couldn't sleep. Was it the different surroundings? Being in someone else's home?

The banging sound grew more severe. It sounded as if someone was trying to break through the downstairs wall.

"Should I get up and check it out?" He thought to himself. "This isn't my house but being a guest shouldn't I be a little responsible if there is an intruder?"

Despite his apartment being in the "not so good" part of town, he never had any problems with someone trying to break in. He had been robbed at gun point on his way home from work one time nine months ago but the robber only got away with the two dollars that were in his wallet.

Surely Todd and Ellen are checking into this sound aren't they? His imagination then took a severe turn. *What if the intruder got to them?* With that thought he got out of bed and walked out of the bedroom into the hall. He decided he would flip on every light switch he could find. Hoping that, if there was an intruder, it might scare them off. *Unless they're the murderous kind of intruder.* He could feel his heart beating faster as he walked down the staircase.

"What have I gotten myself in to?" He mumbled to himself.

He creeped towards the living room. The sound had stopped but the door just before the living room was opening. He looked around for anything he could use as a weapon but he found nothing. Those few seconds watching the door open felt like an eternity to Jeff. "I'm going to die." His overactive imagination kept telling him. Then the door came completely open and it was Ellen, who was extremely startled by Jeff standing there.

"Oh my God Jeff. You about gave me a heart attack." She said after looking confused for a few seconds. Perhaps forgetting that Jeff was there.

"Is everything okay?" Jeff asked. "I heard a pounding sound."

"It was probably just the wind." Ellen said, obviously lying but Jeff couldn't imagine why.

"But... The wind isn't blowing." He said motioning towards the window.

"I'm sorry the sound disturbed you." She said trying to drop the subject and move past to her bedroom.

"It's okay. I was just worried that someone had broken in."

"No. Nothing like that." She said, inching towards her bedroom. "If you will excuse me, Jeff, I am very tired."

The rest of that night Jeff barely slept. When he did he had horrible dreams of someone breaking in and killing everybody in the house. He knew something wasn't right. *Why was Ellen lying about the sound? Why were there two locks on the door?* He thought to himself.

Jeff went down to the kitchen that morning to see Todd and Ellen, apparently, waiting on him with a serious look about them. The only thing that really mattered to him though was the huge breakfast that was prepared on the table. His favorite meal, no matter what time of day. Scrambled eggs, home fries, bacon in bunches, pancakes and *were those croissants? Oh boy, I'm so hungry.* Jeff thought.

Ellen looked up and smiled. "Have a seat Jeff. It's breakfast time."

"Oh my. This looks delicious. What are you guys having?" Jeff asked and then laughed.

After a second or two of laughter from The Matthews, Ellen got a serious look on her face suddenly and almost comically to Jeff. "We need to talk to you about last night." She said

"Is this about the fancy soap in the guest bathroom? I'm sorry, I didn't know they weren't edible." Jeff joked trying to break the tension.

Ellen and Todd laughed for a moment and then Ellen continued. "It's about the sound last night. I think I need to explain."

"It's okay, Ellen, You don't need to explain anything to me. I'm just a guest in your home." Jeff said. He wasn't sure he wanted to have this conversation.

"I feel like I have to be honest with you. You're a very nice guy and you deserve to know. Our... Well... My daughter from my previous marriage lives in the basement and was making the pounding sound."

"Is that all?" Jeff said. Relieved. "I thought you were experimenting on strangers that come to your house after their car had broken down." He joked.

Ellen laughed and continued. "I just didn't want you to think we were bad people."

"Not at all. People live in their parents' basement until they are in their forties nowadays." Jeff said.

"My daughter is ten…."

Jeff was shocked now. *How could they lock a ten year old in the basement? They're crazy. They have to be.* He thought.

"Her name is Rosie and she is a special needs child. She has very violent outbursts at times and it is just safer for her down there." Ellen said uneasily. "We have padded the room so she doesn't get hurt but last night she, somehow got through the padding."

"Oh lord. Is she okay?" Jeff asked genuinely concerned.

"She's fine. She's a tough little girl. She has been through so much." Todd spoke up. Ellen appeared irritated with Todd at this statement. Almost as if he was saying too much.

"Why don't you and Jeff go take a look at his car honey?" She said very abruptly.

About an hour later, after a hearty breakfast, Todd and Jeff went to look at Jeff's car.

"I'm not much of a mechanic but I'm guessing your head gasket is blown." Todd said, with his head deep in the engine.

"Oh man, I'm so screwed." Jeff exclaimed while holding his head with his palms.

He had no idea what to do at this point. He didn't know how to reach his mother, he had no money and he was sure he couldn't stay another night with the Matthews.

"I can take you up to Raven Valley. Mike's Auto can come and pick up your car. I'm pretty sure he even does payment plans." Todd said.

"That would be great." Jeff said while thinking that he may have to get a second job to pay for all of this.

"We should go back to the house and have lunch first." Todd said with a smile. Todd was not one to miss a meal. He enjoyed eating.

On the walk back Todd seemed a little distant, like something was bothering him. He opened his mouth a few times like he was going to say something before he finally started talking.

"She wasn't always like that... Rosie, I mean."

"Oh." Was all Jeff could get out. He really didn't want to talk about this anymore. He just wanted to go home to his little apartment.

"Something happened… She got sick." Todd said, looking at the ground.

"It's really okay Todd. You don't have to explain anything to me. I'm just very grateful for all you and your wife have done for me."

Todd looked a little upset for a minute before smiling, nodding his head and continuing to walk. Maybe he wanted to talk about the situation more. Maybe he felt like he needed someone to talk to about it. Jeff didn't care. He just wanted all of this to be over and to be in his apartment, drinking beer and playing video games by tonight.

They finished lunch which consisted of tuna salad sandwiches, some very salty but good potato chips and what seemed to be cherry Kool-Aid.

"So Jeff, I really need to go out on the farm and check on the animals. If you give me a couple hours I will take you into town." Todd said.

"Sure. Thank you." Jeff said but he really wanted to go now. He had seen enough of country living and just wanted to go home. He knew something strange was going on here as well and didn't want to be a part of any of it.

"Is it okay if I lay down for a few minutes? I didn't sleep well last night." He asked Ellen.

"Absolutely." She said with a smile but there was something different about this smile to Jeff. Almost like she was getting tired of him being there and that was understandable to him.

Jeff laid down and napped for what felt like hours but was actually only about 20 minutes. He looked out the window to see Ellen in the backyard hanging up clothes. There was something peaceful about this to him. Kind of like a simple way of living. He hated going to the Laundromat. *Maybe one day I will settle down and have a simple life like this.* He thought to himself and for the first time that thought brought calm to him.

He walked downstairs and was going into the living room when he just stopped and looked at the door to the basement. He still didn't like that the Matthews kept their daughter in the basement. As much as he wanted to ignore this he could not get it out of his mind. He knew she had to be lonely. Special needs or not.

I have to see her. He said to himself. *She needs human contact.* He wanted to turn away and not care but he couldn't do that. He felt ignored and unwanted, at least by his mother, for too long. Seeing and talking to Rosie was something he felt he needed to do.

He unlocked the top lock. His heart was beating so fast. If they catch me they will be angry. He didn't care. The more he thought about it the more he knew this is what he had to do.

Just as he had unlocked the second lock a big orange cat came out of nowhere scaring the hell out of Jeff. *I didn't even know they had a cat.* He thought to himself, trying to catch his breath. He was undeterred by this as he opened the door.

He was shocked to see a plexi glass screened door at the bottom of the steps. It was secured with padlocks. He would only be able to talk to Rosie through the screen. He closed the door behind him and slowly walked to the bottom of the steps.

There he saw Rosie for the first time. She was crouching in the corner. Her head between her knees. She appeared to be sobbing. *How could anybody do this to a child?*

"Rosie." He called to her. Thinking she was going to look up and have a big smile on her face being so happy to see him.

What he didn't expect was what he saw when she looked up. Her face looked rotted. Her skin was red and looked as if it had been turned inside out. She was baring her teeth and almost growling.

"My God… What the hell?" Was all he could get out before running back up the steps.

He opened the door to see Ellen standing there just as he heard Rosie crashing against the screen door. The welcoming smile on Ellen's face was gone. This was a face of anger.

"Ellen…" He said, trying to find the right words.

"What are you doing Jeff?" She said in a definite irritated tone. "You had no right to go into the basement."

Rosie was shaking the screen door very hard and growling. *Was she really growling?* Jeff could not accept this.

"I just wanted to see her…" Jeff stated. "I thought if I talked to her…"

"Rosie is beyond being talked to." Ellen interrupted. "She's sick Jeff."

"Since you have seen her I will tell you what happened." She continued.

"No… Really there's no need to explain. I will leave and forget this ever happened." Jeff said. He was scared at this point. Ellen was blocking him from going through the door and Rosie was pulling on the screen door so hard it looked as if the hinges were coming loose.

"You have to know the truth." She said very forcefully. "About three years ago, Rosie was playing by the creek while I was hanging clothes, like she always did. After about a half hour she came running up to me crying. She was bitten by what she said looked like a rat. I cleaned up the wound and bandaged it but an hour later her arm around the bandage started getting lesions and they just started spreading so fast. I wanted to get her to a hospital but I was so scared." She started sobbing. Jeff didn't care about this story he just wanted to leave but she continued.

"Rosie began getting violent. Throwing things and screaming which turned into growling. She started towards me and I was terrified. About then her father came in the room. He was a drunken and abusive son of a bitch. Before he knew what was going on Rosie jumped on him and started biting into his flesh. Tearing off chunks and eating them. After a few minutes I grabbed an uneaten piece of his carcass and started pulling it. Luring Rosie into the basement where she has been since."

The screen door was almost off its hinges now. Jeff had only listened to part of the story because he was too worried about Rosie behind him.

"Please Ellen…" He said desperately. "Just let me leave. I won't tell anyone about this."

"Rosie has been very good lately. She had calmed down and stopped trying to get out." She paused for a second and continued. "That is until you showed up."

"Why?" He asked, confused. "Why is my being here affecting her?"

Just after he finished the statement Rosie broke through the screen door and was slowly working on moving past it. Jeff turned and just as he did Ellen pushed Jeff with both hands and he tumbled down the stairs.

"Because she is hungry." Ellen said before closing and locking the basement door.

Todd returned a little while later covered in sweat. He met his wife with a kiss. She was smiling from ear to ear like nothing had happened.

"Is Jeff still asleep?" He asked.

"No." She said, not elaborating.

"Where is he then?" Todd asked as he looked around. He stopped looking and looked into her eyes, realizing. "Again?" He asked "I thought we were going to go into town and pick someone up? I was looking forward to the trip."

"Rosie was hungry." Ellen said with a sly grin.

My Brother Phil

"I keep telling you, my brother Phil did it. It wasn't me." Robbie said to the doctor sitting next to him in the chair.

Robbie was an eight year old little boy who seemed very normal until a few days ago. He sat there and played with the pen he had picked up from the table next to his chair.

"I would like for you to go over this with me again Robbie." The doctor, said. "I don't think you understand how serious this is."

"Why won't anyone believe me? My mommy always taught me to never lie." Robbie said. "I saw Phil do it Dr. Morris. I swear I did."

The doctor looked at Robbie not quite sure what to say next. He had never dealt with a case like Robbie's.

USA Husbands

"Look at this Sue." Mary-Catherine McKenna said to her best friend and neighbor, Sue Westley as they sat on Sue's front porch drinking coffee and reading the newspaper, just as they did every Wednesday morning. "There's a new business in town called USA Husbands. They specialize in training women to be more assertive with their mates."

"Do they take checks?" Sue asked and they both laughed. Their attention was caught by the neighbor across the street. Tess Lohr, who was once again being yelled at, as she left the house to go to work, by her husband, Carl, an alcoholic if there ever was one. Carl had drunk himself out of a job working at the Subaru dealership just across town. He was ten years older than Tess, was balding and showing his beer gut off very well this morning with his, much too form fitting white t-shirt. Sue and Mary-Catherine had noticed the change in Tess and Carl's relationship over the past three years since Carl lost his job. He was never the nicest man before but he had become downright nasty over the years. Sue and Mary-Catherine had been suspecting Carl of abusing Tess for quite some time now. Tess was a little younger than them but they liked Tess. She was down to Earth and, despite the way Carl acted, she was a good wife to him. She worked hard at Benjamin and Farstein, the law firm where she was employed, and often took on several hours of overtime just to keep their family's financial head above water.

"What the hell are you looking at you old bags?!" Carl yelled across the street to them. A funny statement seeing as Carl was a few years older than Sue and Mary-Catherine.

"Good morning to you to you fat drunken asshole." Mary-Catherine mumbled as she waved before turning to talk to Sue. "There is someone who could benefit from USA Husbands."

"Jim is very domineering but that guy..." Sue said, gesturing towards Carl. "... needs to be taught a lesson in how to be more respectful to someone who is supporting him and his alcohol habits."

Mary-Catherine thought about it for a moment and decided she was going to send Tess a text message to ask her if she wanted to drop by later. She was going to confront Tess to see exactly how bad things were with Carl. She felt sad for Tess and almost guilty considering her husband, Rory, was the kindest gentlest man she had ever met. Rory had never so much as raised his voice, let alone a hand, to Mary-Catherine in their twenty-five years of marriage.

Tess accepted Mary-Catherine's invitation and arrived at 9:07pm after Carl had passed out for the evening. They had a pleasant conversation over tea and apple danish, Mary-Catherine's specialty. She felt the time was right to ask Tess a few questions.

"Tess, honey, are things okay between you and Carl?" She asked.

"Well... You know... Not really." Tess replied.

"Has he ever hit you, dear?" Mary-Catherine asked after taking a deep breath. She had known Tess for several years but was still uncomfortable questioning her in this manner.

"Oh no! Never!" Tess replied immediately and Mary-Catherine sensed she was telling the truth. "He's an ass to be sure. He drinks too much, he doesn't look for work, he yells at me and belittles me constantly but he has never so much as raised a hand to me in anger."

"Oh thank God. I would have sent Rory over to beat the stuffing out of him if you had said yes." Mary-Catherine said with a smile. "In that case I think you might benefit from this new company in town called USA Husbands. They have classes that teach you how to be more... uh less dominated."

"Oh I could never do anything like that."

"Yes you could and darlin', you need to do something and quick before he does decide to raise that hand and bring it down to your face." Mary-Catherine said.

"I don't think it would come to that." Tess said and then glanced away. Mary-Catherine could tell the thought had crossed Tess's mind.

"Would it make you feel better if I went with you?" Mary-Catherine queried.

"Why would you go? Rory is great." Tess said.

"Yeah but he could be better." Mary-Catherine laughed.

After a little more coaxing Tess agreed to go to USA Husbands. Mary-Catherine mentioned to Rory that she was going to the classes with Tess, to which he replied: "Whatever you want, dear." without hesitation. Mary-Catherine knew how lucky she was to have a husband like Rory but she was doing this for Tess.

"I want to go too." Sue said as Mary-Catherine was mentioning that she and Tess were going to USA Husbands this evening.

"Yes Sue, you're more than welcome to join." Mary-Catherine said before giving her friend a hug. She couldn't help but smile at Sue's feelings of being left out.

That evening Mary-Catherine, Sue and Tess arrived at USA Husbands and sat in the orientation room. The room was rather large with six rows of three large folding tables facing towards a big screen. They were reading and commenting on the pamphlet they received at the front door highlighting the various courses offered by USA Husbands.

"Here is a course for you Sue." Mary-Catherine said jokingly. ""Building Mr. Perfect". I think I have already mastered that but you could always improve upon Jim."

"Very funny." Sue replied. "That's one of the advanced courses anyway."

A lady wearing a blue dress jacket and matching blue skirt walked to the front of the room.

"If I could have your attention please." She said. "My name is

Jenny Toland. I'm a senior representative for the USA Husbands main branch. I'm going to show you a video now to give you a little insight as to what USA Husbands is all about. Feel free to ask me any questions you may have after the video."

The room went dark and the video began. The video was very dark in content and showed many flashes of, what Mary-Catherine was hoping was re-enactments, of domestic abuse. There were also brief segments of husbands and wife's arguing as well as husbands, obviously, talking down to their wife. Several very brief, dark, flashes of women laying lifeless and often bloody on the ground popped up randomly. The narrator was a female who sounded very nice and comforting. This made Mary-Catherine, oddly, feel even more uneasy.

"Here at USA Husbands, we strive for a better future for wives all over the world. USA Husbands is a company created for women by women. What is the meaning of the name "USA Husbands"? USA is a symbol for freedom. Essentially, the meaning is freedom from the control of your husband. With our easy two week long courses we

provide you with the confidence and the skill set to stand up to that dominating, abusive or lazy husband. Within a matter of months we guarantee you a better life and happier existence or your money back. So take the first step now towards taking back your life. Sign up for your first course now with one of our friendly and helpful representatives. Remember, we're all in this together at USA Husbands. Your happiness is our happiness."

The lights came back on causing everyone in the room to squint.

"Holy shit!" Mary-Catherine said a little louder than she meant to. She as well as Sue and Tess were shocked by the video.

After some questions including a few ridiculous ones, Tess spoke up.

"That video was a little extreme don't you think?" She asked Jenny.

"Extreme?" Jenny replied. She seemed like a sweet person up to this point but Tess's statement seemed to start a fire with the USA Husbands' Representative. "Let me tell you a little story and I will make it short because I'm sure you all are ready to go home now. About ten years ago I was married to a man who drank too much, hit me every time I would even look at him in a manner he didn't approve of and I honestly think he forgot my name because the only thing he called me was "Stupid Bitch". He always insisted on dinner being ready and on the table by 6pm. One day after a particularly long phone conversation with my mother, who was dying of cancer I might add, I noticed it was getting late. I rushed to the kitchen, threw together baked chicken, mashed potatoes and green beans as fast as I could.

I placed the food on the table but he just stared at me. I looked up at the clock and it was 6:05pm. I saw the rage in his eyes and couldn't say a word. He shoved all the food off the table and started punching me in the face before throwing me to the ground and slamming my head on the floor several times until I passed out. I suffered a hemorrhage in my brain and almost died. My jaw had to be wired shut, both of my eyes were swollen shut for a few days and my mother died while I was in the hospital. So now, tell me, was the video too extreme?"

"I'm sorry..." Was all Tess could get out. She was shaken by Jenny's story.

"My point is..." Jenny continued. "... I got out of that pure hell of a marriage and now thanks to USA Husbands, where I am not only an employee but I am also a constant student, I am living a happier life. I just completed the I Control Me, I Control You course and I rule my new husband with an iron fist." With that statement a young lady sitting in the third row spoke up.

"I don't want to rule my husband with an iron fist. I just want him to listen when I talk." She said.

"You can leave now!" Jenny said to her with focused intent. "You're obviously not USA Husbands material. Anyone else who disagrees with our methods or our mission can leave now as well. We are more interested in making the world a better place for women than we are with making money."

The ladies signed up for classes that night. They completed their first two week course, Introduction to a Happier You, followed by the second two week course, Introduction to Pleasing YOU. They learned such things as never letting your husband get the last word, never being afraid he will leave because "you" are better than that and never admit that you are wrong and he is right. Sue took to the courses really well and was happier with Jim than she had been in years. It was at this point that she decided she was no longer going to take classes at USA Husbands.

The next course Mary-Catherine and Tess took without Sue. The course was entitled "Developing Your Own Dominant Personality". Mary-Catherine had no thoughts, anger or regrets about her marriage to Rory until this class. She learned that the only thing she disliked was his passive nature. This wasn't something that the instructor taught. In fact, the instructor taught the class how to instill a passiveness into their husband.

"I would really like it if you weren't so agreeable all the time." Mary-Catherine said to Rory later that night. "It's okay to say no to me or disagree with me once in a while."

"Yes, dear. Whatever you want." Rory replied. Mary-Catherine just rolled her eyes and kissed him on the cheek. She knew she was wasting her time with the classes but she was going to support her friend, Tess.

Tess was feeling very confident. After the first week of the course she decided it was time to take a stand. That night Carl was drunk, as usual. He approached her and started yelling because dinner was not ready yet.

"What the fuck bitch? Where's dinner?" He said to her as she walked in the door. Whether it was Jenny's story or her just being fed up, this statement struck a nerve with Tess.

"I already ate." She said.

"What about me? What am I going to eat?" He asked.

"You're here all day long. You can make your own dinner." She wasn't backing down despite her rapid heartbeat.

"Get in that kitchen and make me something to eat now bitch!" He yelled, pointing towards the kitchen.

"I told you! Make your own dinner!" She said without showing any fear despite her heartbeat now feeling like a race horse going for the finish line inside her chest. She picked up the half drunk bottle of Jack Daniels from the coffee table and threw it at the wall, shattering it into thousands of small shards of glass. "Now listen to me, tomorrow you are going to get off your drunk and lazy ass and look for a job because I am not working myself to the bone to support you doing nothing but drinking anymore."

"And if I don't?" He asked her.

"Try me." She said with a fixed gaze. He started to storm out of the room when she decided to add to the conversation. "And by the way, if you call me bitch again I'm kicking you out of the house. My name is on the mortgage and don't think it won't happen."

He stormed out of the room. Tess was proud of herself. She honestly didn't remember the last time she felt this much pride, this much confidence in herself.

The next day Carl started looking for a job. Within days he had thrown out all of his bottles of alcohol. After two weeks he received a job as a salesman for Temple Ford, a car dealership not far from home.

Shortly after getting the job Carl walked over to Mary-Catherine's porch where her and Sue were having their Wednesday morning coffee/newspaper/gossip session. Mary-Catherine hadn't talked to Tess too much about how things were going with Carl lately. She had noticed that every morning Carl starts Tess's car and holds the door open for her before she leaves for work and prior to leaving for work himself. Tess was also driving a new Ford Fusion and Carl was driving the old, rusty, beaten up car, which was in such bad shape only a car expert would know the make and model. This used to be the car Tess drove and Jim drove his fancy newer model Dodge Ram truck that had seemingly disappeared overnight.

"Good morning ladies. How are you doing this morning?" Carl said. Mary-Catherine and Sue found this very odd. Not just the fact that Carl had hardly said a word to either of them in the past 5 years but also the slow almost defeated tone to Carl's voice.

"We're doing fine, Carl. How are you?" Sue responded.

"I'm doing good. I just wanted to stop by to apologize for the way I acted the last time I spoke to the two of you. I haven't been myself lately." He said. He had a sincere look about him despite sounding as if he was reading what he was saying.

"Apology accepted Carl." Mary-Catherine spoke up. "I'm glad you're feeling better."

"Thank you. If you'll excuse me, I have to get to work. You ladies have a lovely day." He said before walking away.

"Oh my goodness... What has happened to him?" Sue asked Mary-Catherine as she turned to her. "I feel like we just had a conversation with a robot."

"USA Husbands happened to him." Mary-Catherine said.

Later that night Mary-Catherine told Tess that she would not be taking classes at USA Husbands any longer. Tess, who was very loyal to USA Husbands was not too happy.

"Why Mary-Catherine?" She asked.

"I don't need these classes and you are doing so well. You don't need me there with you anymore." Mary-Catherine replied.

"There is so much more to learn though. We can start into the advanced classes soon."

"I haven't gotten a thing from these classes other than further proof that Rory is pretty darn close to perfect." Mary-Catherine said.

"He could be perfect though, Mary-Catherine. There is always room for improvement. You could have him eating out of the palm of your hand." Tess exclaimed. The passion Tess was showing was disturbing Mary-Catherine.

"I'm happy with Rory the way he is." Mary-Catherine said firmly.

Three months later.

"What the hell is this Carl?" Tess said holding up a pair of men's socks.

"A pair of my socks, it looks like." Carl replied.

"They were in my sock drawer!" She yelled.

"I'm sorry honey." He replied.

"I gave you the privilege of washing my clothes and this is how you repay me." She said with a cold tone.

"It won't happen again... Honey... I'm sorry." He said with a tremble.

"Do I need to put you in your place again Carl?"

"No honey." He said, hanging his head.

"Go prepare dinner now, Carl and God help you if you mess anything up." She said to Carl as he walked towards the kitchen.

A few days later Mary-Catherine, Rory, Sue and Jim went over to

Tess and Carl's house for a dinner party. Tess was very lively and talkative. This was a different Tess than Mary-Catherine and Sue were used to seeing. Tess dominated the conversation the entire night. Carl spoke twice. The first time Tess interrupted him. The second time she flat out told him to "Shut up and let the adults talk." Mary-Catherine and Sue were feeling very sorry for Carl. He had been an ass in the past but did not deserve to be degraded in this manner. Rory and Jim, on the other hand, were only concerned about the food, which consisted of chicken wings, chicken fingers, chicken nuggets and tater tots and that was just the appetizers. Carl had prepared a feast. Not to mention, Rory and Jim never really liked Carl.

Suddenly a loud crashing sound came from the kitchen where Carl was working on dinner. Tess rushed to her feet and stormed into the kitchen. Whether she didn't care or didn't know that she was yelling loud enough for the others to hear Mary-Catherine wasn't sure.

"OH CARL! AN ENTIRE PAN OF ROLLS! YOU STUPID USELESS SON OF A BITCH!" Tess yelled.

"I'm sorry honey. I burned my hand." Carl replied.

"I don't give a shit Carl. We have guests and you're embarrassing me." She continued. "You think you're little hand hurts do you?"

A loud scream resonated through the room that made Rory and Jim actually look up from their food momentarily. Mary-Catherine and Sue looked at each other with worry. They didn't know what happened to their sweet friend Tess. Had she snapped? Did Carl push her too far with his drinking?

"I'm sorry. My husband is being unbearable as usual." Tess said as she was coming from the kitchen. Everyone was speechless.

Carl didn't return for dinner or the after dinner conversation that Mary-Catherine and Sue wanted to escape terribly. Rory and Jim ate dessert and then more dessert. Between the appetizers, the steak, baked potatoes, corn on the cob, carrot cake, apple pie, cherry pie and ice cream Rory and Jim consumed, Mary-Catherine assumed her and Sue would have to roll them home. Mary-Catherine was concerned about Carl and excused herself, saying she had to visit the little girl's room.

She passed the master bedroom along the way where she heard Carl softy weeping. She almost walked on but her busybody habits wouldn't let her. She knocked on the partially opened door.

"Carl." She whispered. "Are you alright?"

"Yes. I'm fine. Thank you." He replied.

"You don't sound fine. What's wrong?" She asked.

"Nothing. I'm okay Mary-Catherine." He said. She knew he wasn't okay and walked in the bedroom. He tried to turn his back to her but she was having none of it. She turned him around and was shocked by the large burn on his forehead and right forearm.

"My God Carl."

"It's nothing." He said, wincing in pain as she touched his forehead. "I'm just... clumsy."

"Bullshit Carl." She said matter-of-factly. "She did this to you."

"She just gets mad sometimes. It's my fault." He said as he started crying again.

"This is not your fault. Tess is out of control." Mary-Catherine said.

"Please don't tell her you talked to me." He said.

"Carl..."

"Please... Don't tell her." He said and then looked around, thinking he was speaking too loud.

Mary-Catherine agreed not to say anything to Tess but she was going to grab Rory and leave. She walked into the living room where Tess was telling Sue about her latest class "Cracking the Whip".

"Rory I think we should leave." Mary-Catherine said.

"I'm still eating." Rory said. His mouth full of apple pie.

"For God's sake Rory you have had enough food for one night." She said.

"Is everything okay Mary-Catherine?" Tess asked.

"Yes. I'm just... feeling... not so well." Mary-Catherine responded. She really wasn't feeling so well after seeing Carl's burns.

Rory stared, with his head down, at the piece of apple pie on his plate, his mouth still full.

"It's okay Rory. You can take the rest of the pie with you." Tess stated.

"Can I take the cherry pie?" Jim asked with a child-like smile.

"Of course." Tess replied.

The neighbors all left together. Tess immediately went to the master bedroom.

"You told her didn't you." She said to Carl, who was sitting on the edge of the bed. "You're night just got worse Carl."

"Looks like Carl is finally off of those crutches." Mary-Catherine said to Sue as Sue was sipping her Wednesday morning coffee.

"I didn't think a car salesman was such a risky job." Sue replied.

"Tess said he slipped on the wet floor in his office." Mary-Catherine said skeptically.

"Why do you sound like you don't believe that?" Sue said.

"Have you seen Rory's new Ford truck?" Mary-Catherine asked.

"Yes. It's very nice." Sue said as she took another sip of her coffee.

"Carl sold it to him."

"Okay?" Sue said, not sure where she was going with this.

"Carl has carpet in his office. In fact the entire building is carpeted." Mary-Catherine continued.

"What are you saying Mary-Catherine?"

"Open your eyes Sue. Tess did something to him." Mary-Catherine said not understanding why her friend wasn't getting it.

"Tess? She's just a little thing." Sue said while laughing.

"Have you not been seeing what's going on over there Sue? What about the night of the dinner party. All the burns." Mary-Catherine said.

"Carl even said himself that he tripped and fell on the oven."

Mary-Catherine knew she was getting nowhere with Sue. Sue, despite only taking a couple of classes was a staunch supporter of USA Husbands. She felt like they "saved her marriage". Mary-Catherine thought that statement was very dramatic. In all the years she had known Sue and Jim she had never seen them have a single argument or either one be mean to the other.

"Everything okay Carl?" Jack Mooneyham, the senior sales

associate at Temple Ford, asked Carl as he walked into his office and saw him slumped over in his chair."

"Yes... Everything is great Jack." He said as he looked up, startled.

"You don't look so good buddy."

"I'm sorry. I just haven't been sleeping well lately." Carl replied.

"You're doing a great job here Carl. I just wanted you to know that. We haven't had anyone sell this many cars in years. Not since Dave Butcherman and that bastard left us for Nguyen Chevrolet. Please don't do that." Jack said.

"No need to worry. I like it here." Carl replied.

Jack was pleased with his response. He smiled and walked away. Carl was a little worried that Jack saw through his facade. He was just having so much trouble handling his home life. The only time he was remotely happy was at work. He walked on egg shells at home.

Always afraid he was going to say the wrong thing or look at her wrong.

"Maybe I really do deserve this." He thought to himself. "I was such a mean drunk."

He had secretly been putting money back from bonuses he had received for a job well done. He knew the time may come when he may need to get away. He just hoped his old clunker would get him at least to an airport.

About six o'clock, Carl walked into the house and immediately felt as if something was wrong. There was an eerie feel. Tess's car was outside but she was not in her usual spot on the couch. He walked into the kitchen and there she stood by the sink, arms folded and glaring at him.

"Hey honey," He said to her.

"I want you to open this drawer." She said, pointing at the drawer to the left of the sink.

Carl opened the drawer which contained the envelope full of money he had hidden away.

"I can explain honey." He said, obviously frightened.

"I found this behind a loose panel in the basement behind your toolbox. Why was it there Carl?!" She was getting angrier by the second.

"I was saving it to buy you something... something nice." He lied hoping she would believe.

"I don't need a man to buy me anything. I buy what I want, when I want for me..." She said.

"I know... I'm sorry..."

"How many times have I told you. You bring any money you make directly to me. You DO NOT get to keep money for yourself." She said with a fire in her eyes. Carl looked at the ground not sure what was coming for him next.

"Now open this drawer." She said pointing to the drawer on the right side of the sink. Carl looked in the drawer and gasped.

The next morning, Wednesday morning, Mary-Catherine and Sue sat on the porch with their coffee and newspaper. They watched as Carl started Tess's car and saw her off to work as he did every morning, even while he was on crutches.

"They look happy." Sue said as Carl kissed Tess on the cheek.

"Whatever you say Sue." Mary-Catherine said, not wanting another debate.

Carl looked in the direction of Mary-Catherine and Sue. They waved at him in unison. He waved back. Mary-Catherine and Sue's faces both froze in fear as they noticed his bandaged hand simultaneously.

"Oh my God he's missing two fingers." Sue said in horror.

A week went by and they hadn't seen Carl leave the house since the previous Wednesday morning. That afternoon Mary-Catherine noticed Carl's car was gone. She decided she was going to confront Tess tonight when Tess returned from work. The cruel and unusual lessons USA Husbands was teaching had gone too far.

Tess returned home from work at roughly 5:30pm. Mary-Catherine was waiting on Tess's porch for her.

"Well Mary-Catherine. What a nice surprise." Tess said with a smile.

"We need to talk Tess." Mary-Catherine said in a very serious manner.

"About?"

"You and Carl." Mary-Catherine replied.

"Nothing to talk about. I have never been so happy." Tess said with a smirk.

"Knock it off Tess!" Mary-Catherine said with anger building up within her. Tess's attitude was making her boil inside. "I know what's going on."

"And what is going on Mary-Catherine?" Tess said, still smirking.

"You have been hurting Carl." Mary-Catherine stated.

"Oh yes. Big bad Tess is hurting little Carl." Tess laughed.

"I can see what you are doing Tess. The night of the dinner party,

Carl on crutches saying he slipped on the wet floor at work when his work is all carpeted, have you even been there? Then, this morning..." Mary-Catherine took a deep breath before continuing. "When he waved... we saw he was missing his index and middle finger on his right hand."

"He's clumsy and accident prone..." Tess said, smirking.

Before she even realized what she was doing, Mary-Catherine reached out and slapped Tess across the face so hard she fell to the ground.

"What the hell is your problem?" Tess asked as she was getting up from the ground. Mary-Catherine knew she shouldn't have hit Tess. Violence was not going to settle a problem with violence. Tess needed to be brought back down to earth though.

"Carl was bad to you when he was drinking but what you're doing is not right Tess." Mary-Catherine said.

"I haven't done anything to him. How dare you accuse me of such a thing?"

"You're forgetting I used to take the classes at USA Husbands. I remember the courses about using their words against them, that flowing into learning to control with your own words and I also remember the "Self-defense" course and how they implied using the techniques to control your spouse. USA Husbands is a bad, bad place Tess. They have brainwashed you. You used to be a sweet thing." Mary-Catherine said, not breaking eye contact.

"Oh my God Mary-Catherine! Wake up! I was so weak before USA Husbands. They turned my life around. They made me strong and confident." Tess said almost as if she were in the orientation video.

"I'm strong and confident Tess but the difference is, I don't have to be violent with my husband." Mary-Catherine stated.

"Well good for you Mary-Catherine." Tess said sarcastically. "Not all of us are as lucky as you. If I hadn't taken a stand Carl would still be putting me down every chance he got and eventually would have started hitting me and the old Tess would have just taken it. Well the new Tess doesn't take shit. The new Tess strikes first."

"Listen to yourself." Mary-Catherine said, frustrated. "You sound just like the advertisements for that damn place. You're going down a dark road Tess. I love you and I want to help you but you have to stop with these classes."

"I only have one more class. I'm not stopping." Tess said.

"You have to stop Tess before USA Husbands takes the rest of who you are. Being strong and confident is one thing but becoming what you're becoming is something very bad."

"Look, Mary-Catherine, I have one more class. Everything will be complete when it is over. I will have taken control of my life. I have to finish this out."

Mary-Catherine felt she had done all she could for now. She hoped she had gotten through to Tess at least a little. Hopefully some of the old Tess was still within her. Maybe after the classes were done Tess would feel fulfilled and not continue her current behavior.

She walked past Tess's car and noticed an envelope on the ground next to the black Ford Fusion. She picked it up, saw the USA Husbands logo and shoved it in her pocket. She took the envelope back to her house, went into the kitchen and read the form. Which stated: Congratulations on completing your latest course "Proper Disposal of the Body" we are pleased to see you have signed up for the follow up course "Moving On To the Next Husband".

The Tree on Top of the Hill

Jim Farance and Corey Gates approached the dirt road. They had been walking through the woods during their hunting expedition for hours. The somewhat level dirt road seemed like a treat at this point. Jim was an avid hunter, coming out to this same area every year. Corey, on the other hand, was hunting for the very first time. Jim and Corey had met only three weeks earlier. Corey had just started working at Graves' Chemical, a large factory in town that processes polymer. Corey was new to the small town of Elk's Grove and has been considered a city slicker most of his life. Jim, feeling sorry for Corey who was known by other workers at the plant as "City Boy", decided to befriend Corey and invited him and his wife to Thanksgiving dinner. Thanksgiving at the Farance house always included Jim's wife, Marie and his mother making dinner while Jim and his father went hunting. Jim's father had passed away earlier in the year and Jim was going to skip the hunting this season until he invited Corey, who initially declined until Kelly, his wife, urged him to go along, she wanted him to have friends.

"You know, it sounds funny, but I have never even seen a dirt road first hand." Corey said, kind of embarrassed at this statement.

"Plenty of dirt roads in Elk's Grove and I have probably been on them all." Jim replied.

They approached a large hill just off the dirt road. The hill looked out of place as the grass was still green despite the fact that there had been snow at least three times since fall had started.

"Wow... This is like something you would see in a painting." Corey said as he gazed upon the field, his vision resting on the large tree at the top of the hill. The tree, actually the only tree on this hill, looked as if it had been dead for quite some time but stood out so well with the green grass.

Corey decided he wanted a better look at the tree so he took out his binoculars. Before he could get the binoculars to his eyes Jim put his hand on them to stop him.

"Whoa! What are you doing?" Jim asked.

"I'm just trying to get a better look at that big tree." He replied.

"Probably not a good idea." Jim said very seriously.

"Why not?"

"There's this thing about the tree on the hill... Probably just an urban legend but, personally, I don't want to take the chance." Jim responded.

"An urban legend? About a tree?" Corey asked with a slight giggle, thinking this was just another stupid small town thing. He really hated the small town scene but his wife loved it and that was what was important to him."

"Let's just not worry about it. I would really just rather you not look at the tree." Jim said.

"What is the urban legend about?" Corey asked with a smirk.

"Well..." Jim started before taking a small pause. "From what I had heard about it, looking with the naked eye at the tree you are fine, going up to the tree, leaning against it, doing whatever you want is fine but if you look at it from a distance through, say, binoculars something happens."

"What do you mean something happens?" Corey asked.

"Like I said, I'm going on what I have heard. People say if you look at the tree through binoculars, you see something else... They say it's something so scary and terrifying that it causes even the strongest of minds to go insane. Most people have killed themselves in this very spot, binoculars lying next to them." Jim stated.

Corey looked at him for a second and started laughing.

"That's a good one man, you had me going for a second. Even

gave me a little chill down my spine." He said.

"I'm just telling you what I have heard." Jim said in a straight forward tone.

"I know I'm the new guy in town and it's cool that you want to pull a rib on me." Corey said.

"No man, this is not a rib. Call me superstitious but I wouldn't look at the tree with those binoculars if someone paid me." Jim said.

"You don't seem the type to be afraid of a little urban legend." Corey said.

"If a bear came darting out of the woods at us right now, I probably wouldn't even flinch but there's just certain things I don't mess with." Jim replied.

"I don't believe in urban legends but if a bear came out of the woods right now I would piss myself without hesitation." Corey said, Jim laughed. He liked Corey, he liked Corey's sense of humor.

"That being said. Can we move on?" Jim asked.

"I still would like to look at the tree a little better." Corey said.

"Walk up there then."

"That's a pretty steep hill I don't want to climb it. I'll use my binoculars. I'll be fine." Corey said as he started to bring the binoculars to his eyes. Jim stopped him again, this time more forcibly.

"Please don't do that." Jim said, staring into Corey's eyes with intent.

"What's your problem man?" Corey said, a little taken back. Jim was no small man but Corey was average size. He knew if there was a problem he wouldn't be able to fight Jim off but his curiosity was killing him now.

"Clois Bonner..." Jim said.

"What?" Corey asked, confused.

"She used to live in the house just up the road from me." Jim responded.

"Okay?"

"She lives in a mental institution now. From what I heard she was found out here laying on the ground in the fetal position trembling. That was ten years ago and from what I have heard the only thing she has said since then is 'Dear God help me.' Don't do this Corey." Jim said. He looked scared.

"Just let me entertain my curiosity here, Jim. I take full responsibility." Corey said. He was not believing any of this. He truly felt like Jim was pulling a gag on him. Cloris Leachman? Or whatever her name was. Come on, how did Jim's small town brain come up with a name that quick.

"Don't do it Corey... Do you want me to beg?" Jim said. Corey appreciated how far he was going with the joke but even if it wasn't a trick and Jim really was serious, Corey really had to look now. He couldn't help himself.

"Stop it Jim." Corey said, shrugging Jim off. He tried pushing him away but moving Jim was like moving a mountain. "I'm the one looking at the tree. Why are you so scared?"

"I don't want to go back and tell your wife what happened, first of all and I just don't want something bad to happen." Jim said.

"Nothing bad is going to happen. I just want to look at the tree then we can move on." Corey said. Corey thought to himself that this compulsion to look at the tree was a strange feeling. He was always a strong willed person but usually not to this degree.

"God dammit man." Jim said. He was scared but he knew Corey was going to look at the tree, if not today then another day. He was going to have to let it happen and deal with the consequences. As much as Corey believed the legend was false, Jim believed ten times more that it was true.

Corey stepped back, looked at Jim for a second, sure that he was going to try to stop him again but Jim just stood there with his hands held tight behind his head as if he was bracing himself for an impact.

Corey put the binoculars to his eyes and almost immediately Jim could tell something was wrong. Corey's entire face reacted in terror. He let out a terrible gasp and screamed. The scream was blood curdling. Jim had never heard a man scream before but he knew if he had this would be the worst scream he could have heard. The scream brought terror to Jim who was starting towards Corey now.

"Oh Jesus... Oh God... Please! No!" Corey said with so much fear in his voice.

"Oh God... What is it man?" Jim asked frantically.

"JESUS, GOD ALMIGHTY JIM... JESUS, GOD ALMIGHTY!" Corey said. He threw the binoculars down and started clawing at his face bringing blood.

Jim walked over to Corey, grabbed him by the shoulders and was going to lay him on the ground but Corey pushed him off with a fury and power that Jim didn't expect. Jim fell to the ground and gazed upon Corey in horror. He had scratched off a good portion of the skin on his face and was bleeding profusely. Corey looked down at the rifle he had borrowed from Jim. He reached down to pick it up. Before Jim could get to his feet, Corey put the rifle under his chin and pulled the trigger.

The Bad Daddy

Jared Graham sat at the breakfast table with his 8 year old daughter, Toni, talking about what they were going to do today. Jared was drinking his coffee while Toni was drinking her juice from a coffee cup pretending she was drinking coffee. Her father was her "favorite person on Earth," she always told everyone who would listen. She wanted to be just like him when she grew up. Jared was honestly hoping she would strive for better. He was not happy with his job as senior sales associate at Whitmeyer and Nathan, a public trading company, and had not been for years, but it was what kept the family afloat.

This was the best part of the day for Jared. He loved spending any time he could with his little girl. She was always so loving towards him and so entertaining when she talked about something for which she had passion.

"So, Rachel and I have planned to meet under the monkey bars somewhere around twelvish. From there we are going to go to the swing sets where we will spend the rest of our recess." Toni said in such a serious manner that it caused an eruption of laughter from Jared.

"Eat your cereal baby." Jared said to her. "It sounds like you have a busy day ahead of you. You'll need your strength."

"I know. Third grade is so tiring." She said. Jared wondered if it got any better than these moments with Toni.

"Toni, honey. The bus is here." The voice came from the living room.

"Coming Mommy." Toni yelled back. She kissed her father on the cheek and went running to the bus, stopping just for a second to give her mom a kiss.

"Love you Mommy." She said and ran out the door.

"Love you too Sweetie." Megan Graham replied.

Jared sat at the table for a few minutes and contemplated his day. He had yet another boring sales associate's meeting to oversee this afternoon, but he needed to duck out early. He had to stop by North Side Continuous Care. It had been a few weeks since he had visited. Today seemed like as good as any.

"So, you're going to see Jill today?" Megan said as she walked in the room. She was still sweaty from her morning run with Fester, Toni's three year old golden lab. Her runs with Fester are never meant to be a workout. Fester will usually pick up on a scent and Megan is forced to go along for some cardio training.

"Yeah. It's been a few weeks. I feel like I should." He replied.

"Okay." She said, in a slightly upset manner.

"You should come." He said to her.

"I would really rather not." Megan said in a little more even tone.

Jill was Jared's first wife. Three years after they were married, Jill had a car accident that she barely survived. She had been in a coma since the accident. Jared was going to visit a few times a week until about two years ago because he knew it upset Megan and he loved Megan so much that he couldn't stand seeing her hurt. Jill had been in a very bad facility that was shut down not long after she was moved to North Side. She would get infections regularly, and nearly died on several occasions.

More than anything, Megan had feelings of guilt concerning Jill. She had been Jill's best friend. Megan and Jared had not even the slightest attraction to each other before Jill's accident. Before her and Jared started seeing each other, Jill's parents considered Megan part of the family. They now would say anything they could to make Megan feel guilty for marrying their daughter's husband, often leaving Megan in tears.

That afternoon, Jared visited Jill. It bothered Jared how bad she looked. Apparently, since he last visited, she had to have surgery to remove an aneurysm in her brain. Her head had been shaved and was bandaged. One of the things that had attracted Jared to Jill when they met in college all those years ago was her long flowing blonde hair, which she had retained through this entire ordeal until now.

On his way home Jared, despite every effort to hold it back, wept softly. He hated seeing Jill like this. He felt so guilty, but couldn't help thinking she would be better off if she would just let go of life.

When he returned home Megan was apologetic over their conversation this morning.

"I'm sorry, I just feel so bad sometimes. I feel like I stole my best friend's husband." She told Jared through tears. "I feel guilty every time Toni calls me mommy."

Toni was two years old when Jill had the accident. They had made sure that Toni knew that Megan was not her real mother, but Toni thought of Megan as her mother anyway, and Megan loved her so much. They had told Toni that her mother had passed away shortly after the accident, so as not to upset her. With the fact that Jill's family wanted nothing to do with Toni, it made the lie easier to uphold.

"It's okay honey. You are allowed to be upset. I'm sure this was not what you had in mind when you used to dream about meeting the perfect guy..." He said, puffing out his chest jokingly. "... and living happily ever after, but Toni and I both love you terribly. She thinks of you as her mommy and so do I."

That night Jared had terrible dreams and they all concerned Jill. She was blaming him for her death. It wasn't playing into Jared's usual guilt. He felt guilty because Jill was on her way to pick Toni up from the babysitter's house, a task that Jared was supposed to do, but he had called Jill earlier in the day to ask her if she would pick Toni up. He told her he had to work late, but was actually going to have a few drinks with his best friend Kyle.

The next morning, while Megan was out running with Fester, Jared tried to have his normal breakfast conversation with Toni, but she was very lethargic and not talking much.

"What's wrong honey? Did you not sleep well?" He asked her after she had ignored his third attempt to rope her into a conversation.

"I didn't sleep good at all Daddy." She said, yawning.

"Why not? Too many things that you wanted to do today on your mind?" He asked. Yes he was still trying to get the conversation going. He needed it to get through his day.

"You know why I couldn't sleep Daddy." She said, her eyes closed, resting her head on her hand.

"I do?"

"Yes you do." She responded in an uncharacteristically snippy tone.

"I don't honey. Why didn't you sleep well?" He asked.

"Because you were standing in my doorway almost all night." She said.

"Honey, you must have been dreaming. I wasn't in your doorway." He said.

"I wasn't dreaming. I was awake. I asked you why you were standing there and you didn't answer me." She said before getting up and running to the bus. The bus driver had blown the bus horn halfway through her sentence. She hadn't even stopped to kiss him goodbye.

Jared sat in confusion. He hadn't left his and Megan's bed all night.

"Maybe you were sleepwalking." Megan said when he told her about the conversation with Toni.

"I don't think I have ever sleepwalked." He responded.

"Maybe you should call your mom. You may have been a sleepwalker as a child and it started again." Megan said while buttering a piece of wheat toast.

"She's in Vegas again. I'll call her when she gets back."

"She's such an outgoing gambler." Megan laughed.

Jared sat in his office that afternoon with a shaky feeling inside that he couldn't quite understand and couldn't escape. There was something about Toni's statement that sent chills through him, though he didn't know why. He knew there had to be a logical explanation, like him sleepwalking, but he still had a bad feeling.

That night Toni was sleeping very soundly. She had been tired all day from not sleeping well the previous night. She was having a dream about running around in the backyard with Fester. She was throwing a tennis ball to him. The ball went into the bushes, when

Fester brought the ball back he dropped it in her hand, like he always had, but this time it wasn't a tennis ball. It was a human eye that was covered in maggots." She woke up suddenly and almost screamed until she saw Jared standing next to her bed. She was comforted by his presence.

"Daddy, I had a bad dream." She said, fighting back tears.

Jared didn't say a word and stared at her. She reached out and hugged him. Jeff didn't return the embrace.

"Daddy?" She asked in a frightened tone. She had hugged her father so many times, but this just didn't feel right. This didn't feel like she was hugging her father. She let him go and screamed. The man she thought was her father walked out of the room and down the hallway. About thirty seconds later Jared ran, with intent, into Toni's room.

"What is it baby?" He asked, looking around the room.

"You scared me Daddy." She said, crying. "I hugged you, but it wasn't you. Why did you do that?"

"Slow down honey. What are you talking about?" He asked, confused.

"I... had a bad dream." She said, trying to catch her breath. "I woke up and you were standing there. You weren't you though."

"It's okay honey. It was just a dream." He told her, pressing her head into his chest.

"It wasn't a dream Daddy." She said.

Jared walked into the bedroom and stood in front of Megan.

"Is everything okay?" She asked him. He stood there staring at her and didn't respond.

"Jared? Did you hear me?" She asked. Still no response.

Jared began to lick his fingers and then pointed directly at Megan.

"Jared, what the hell has gotten into you?" She said. Jared still didn't respond. He walked into the bathroom that was attached to the master bathroom and closed the door.

"Who are you talking to?" Jared said as he walked into the bedroom from the hallway.

"What kind of trick are you trying to pull?" She asked him. "Toni is screaming for you and you're pulling tricks."

"Sweetheart, what do you mean?" He asked, puzzled.

"Cut the crap Jared. You came in. I asked if Toni was alright, you didn't answer me. Then you walked into the bathroom."

"Daddy was with me Mommy." Toni said, coming from behind Jared.

"You were here..." Megan continued. "You just walked into the bathroom... How did you get to the hallway?"

Jared went into the bathroom. While he was in there Toni looked at Megan and said:

"That was the bad Daddy." Toni's words sent chills down Megan's spine.

Jared found nothing in the bathroom. They all slept, very uncomfortably, in the living room that night. Jared stretched out in a recliner with Megan in the other that she had butted up against Jared's chair. Toni slept on the couch, next to Fester, who had been suspiciously quiet throughout the incident upstairs. Normally he took any opportunity he could to bark.

They decided it would be best for Toni to stay home from school the next day. Megan didn't want to be at the house with Jared not there so she and Toni went to Megan's mother's house.

Jared had a very long day. He couldn't concentrate at work and his drive home seemed to take a lifetime. When he got home he received a call from his friend Kyle.

"You're a fucking jackass." Were Kyle's first words. He had said it in a joking manner, but given the past day's events Jared took offense.

"What the hell are you talking about?" Jared asked in an irritated tone.

"I haven't seen you in two years and when I finally do you ignore me." Kyle stated. Kyle lived two states from Jared and they hadn't seen each other in quite some time. "What? Were you in town for one of your little meetings?"

"I haven't so much as left town in two months." Jared said.

"Yeah whatever man. I know my best bud when I see him." Kyle said.

"Kyle I wasn't there." Jared said. He was getting annoyed with Kyle.

"Dude. You were totally here. I was in Walmart. You passed me in the electronics section. I was like 'Hey man what are you doing here?' and you ignored me and kept walking. I tried to keep up, but I lost sight of you." Kyle said.

He would feel bad about it later, but he hung up the phone suddenly. He was very distraught at this point.

"What the hell is going on?" He yelled.

The phone rang again. He was expecting it to be Megan but it was Susie from North Side.

"Jared? This is Susie from North Side." She said.

"Hey Susie. What's up?" Jared asked. Jared had been friendly with Susie as she was Jill's nurse on most occasions.

"I'm afraid I have bad news." She said. Jared gulped. He knew what was coming. "Jill has passed away." Jared felt sorrow, but also felt relief at the same time.

"Oh my God." Jared said, fighting back tears. "Well thank you for letting me know Susie."

"There's more Jared." She said. "Jill awoke from her coma briefly before she died."

"Really?"

"She woke up let out a scream and then she was gone. It happened shortly after you left." She added.

"You're just now telling me." He said. A little upset he was just now hearing the news.

"I'm sorry Jared, but that was only an hour ago." She said.

"Of course... I apologize Susie." Jared said before hanging up. He knew he hadn't been to see Jill in two days, but with the weird occurrences that were going on, he didn't mention that to Susie.

He frantically called Megan and told her to stay at her mother's with Toni for the time being. He hadn't mentioned Jill's death. There was so much happening. He was scared. He actually wished that they hadn't taken Fester to Megan's mother's house, he would have provided some comfort.

"Mom? Do you have time to talk?" He asked his mother. He wasn't going to call her while she was on vacation, but felt he needed to talk to her. She was always willing to talk through his problems with him.

"Of course Jared. What's up? She asked.

"For starters I just found out Jill died." He said, causing his mother to gasp. She would never say anything, but she always liked Jill better than Megan. Megan was good to Jared and she appreciated that, but she looked at Megan as an opportunist. She felt as if Megan wanted Jared even before Jill's accident and waited for the opportunity to move in on him. "There's something else and I'm not sure how to say this."

"What is it Jared?" She asked.

"It's really weird. I don't know how to say this."

"Just say it Jared." She said matter-of-factly.

"There seems to be another me that everyone is seeing." He said. She was silent. "He looks just like me and the worst thing is that he has been in my house." She was silent for a moment.

"Oh God Jared." She said, breaking her silence.

"I know it's crazy but..." Jared said before his mother interrupted...

"I should have told you this years ago..." She said before Jared returned the interruption.

"Should have told me what?"

"When you were five, I went into your room one night around three in the morning because I had awakened with a bad feeling. I opened the door and saw a child standing beside your bed. I spoke to him, but he didn't answer. I walked up to him to where I could see his face..." She hesitated for a moment before continuing. "It was you Jared."

"Oh Jesus Mom." Jared said.

"I never told your father. He would have had me committed." She continued.

"Was that the only time?" He asked. Holding his head in his hands.

"There were a few more times. Once when you were seven, he was standing behind you while you were playing in the backyard. About a year later I saw him in the basement while you were at school. I didn't see him for several years until one of your high school basketball games. He was standing next to the emergency exit next to the bleachers." She said.

"Did he ever say anything to you?" He asked.

"No. Never." She responded.

Jared held his breath as he glanced at the kitchen window. It was dark, but he could make him out clearly. He had seen him, seen the other him for the first time as he passed the window. Jared ran to the front door and circled around the house twice, but couldn't find him.

Megan jumped when she heard the knock at the door. She and Toni looked out the window to the side of the front door to see Jared knocking. Megan turned and started to go for the door before Toni stopped her.

"No Mommy." She said. "That's the bad Daddy."

"How do you know?" Megan asked her.

"His eyes. They aren't the same as Daddy's." She replied.

Before they knew it and before Megan could stop her, Megan's mother opened the door. She smiled when she saw Jared, but it wasn't quite Jared. He grabbed her by the throat and threw her against the wall. She slumped to the floor a dark red streak of blood followed her down the wall.

Toni screamed and they ran through the house to the back door in the kitchen. They reached the car, got inside and Megan started the car. They had gone two blocks before Megan realized something wasn't right and at that moment he popped up in the back seat. She could see his face in the rear view mirror and knew what Toni meant. His eyes were different than the good Jared's. They were the same shape and they each had brown eyes, but there was something more sinister in the eyes of the man in the back seat. Megan and Toni both screamed. The man grabbed Toni and was trying to pull her into the back seat, but her seat belt held her in place. Megan tried hitting the man who didn't even register the blows.

Megan was struggling to keep the car under control. She was swerving from side to side while fighting with the man, who was still grabbing Toni. She nearly hit a car in the opposite lane. If the car had not swerved into what should have been the lane Megan was in they would have collided head on. Megan slammed on the brakes sending the man head first into the windshield, which didn't break. The force had sent the man into the front seat with them.

"Toni, get your seat belt off quick and get out." Megan said.

The man was startled and barely moving. Megan pulled Toni to the side of the road. She went back to the car and retrieved an umbrella from under the seat. She hit the man a few times with it, as he was starting to reach for her. She fixed the umbrella to the gas pedal so that the engine was revved up before putting the car in gear. The car was moving as fast as a mid-size sedan could go before it hit the side of the big brick building that had been empty since the five and dime closed in the eighties. The car burst into flames and Megan breathed a sigh of relief.

She held Toni tight, then made sure she was okay before calling Jared.

"It's over." She said to him, still crying. "The car... it hit the building... He's dead."

"Oh my God honey. Are you and Toni alright." He said frantically.

"Yes. We're fine. We're going back to my mom's. I think she might be hurt." Megan said crying harder.

"I'll come over there." He said.

Jared arrived an hour later to find that Megan's mother had died immediately after hitting the wall. Megan had not known what to tell the police. "My husband's doppelganger killed my mother." didn't seem like something they would believe.

"So the stranger threw your mother against the wall, stole your car keys from the table next to the door and took your car is your statement ma'am?" Detective John Reyes asked Megan.

"Yes sir." She said. She was still shaken up.

"The man was obviously on something. He hit a building about a half mile down the street. I don't even think we'll be able to identify the body." He added.

They decided to stay at Megan's mother's house that night. Megan was so distraught that she couldn't sleep until she had taken a sedative she found in her mother's medicine cabinet. Jared could not sleep at all. He just kept running through the events of the past few days in his head. He was relieved it was over. He knew it was going to take a lot of time to return to a normal life, but knew they would get there together as a family.

He tossed and turned a few more times before getting up to go to the bathroom down the hall. He washed his face and was drying it with a towel when he looked into the mirror and almost fell over in shock. Behind his reflection in the mirror stood Jill. She looked just as she had before the accident. There were no facial scars and her long blonde hair was back.

"Don't turn around Jared." She said. "If you do I will be gone."

"My God... Jill." He said with baited breath.

"I need to tell you something." She continued. "I blamed you for so many years for my accident..."

"I'm so sorry... I should have picked Toni up that day." He

interrupted.

"Just listen to me Jared." She said, as assertive as she always was. "The reason I blamed you is because just before the accident you came out of the back seat and wrapped a cord around my neck and started choking me..."

"What, my God Jill... No... I never would have..." He said with terror.

"I know it wasn't you... I know now. He came to the home and even though the nurse said it was you there to see me I knew by his presence that it wasn't you. There was just a dark and evil feeling about him that I hadn't noticed before. I had seen him before the night of the accident many times and thought it was you, I realized this just before he smothered me with the pillow." She said.

"I'm so sorry Jill... I should have been there." He said.

"Everything is okay Jared. You have your family to think about.

It's me that should be sorry. I should have moved on long ago instead of tying you up emotionally." She said.

"There's no need to be sorry Jill."

"You need to take care of Megan and Toni, they're not safe." Jill said.

"He's dead... The guy... the other me." He said.

"It's not over Jared..." Before she could continue Jared saw the reflection of the other him come up from behind Jill and he was frozen in fear. The guy grabbed Jill by her long blonde hair, pulled it back and slit her throat with a large butcher knife.

When Jared turned around Jill was gone but the man stood there holding the butcher knife.

"Is everything okay Jared?!" Megan yelled as she was running down the hall.

The man slowly reached over and locked the door. He thrust the knife at Jared, who grabbed his arm. Jared struggled with the other him. Who was much stronger than he was. He slammed Jared against the wall and tried to shove the knife into Jared's chest. Jared extended his leg and kicked the man between the legs sending him back. Jared punched him in the face as hard as he could, but the man was unrelenting. He grabbed the big ceramic cover to the back of the toilet but the man shook the blow off.

"Mommy? What's Daddy doing?" Toni asked as she approached Megan who was still trying, desperately to open the bathroom door.

She grabbed Toni and hugged her. She knew there was nothing she could do. She only hoped that Jared could win this fight against himself.

"It's okay sweetie. Daddy is going to be fine." Megan said to Toni, still holding her.

The banging and crashing only seemed to intensify. It seemed like hours, but the fight only lasted a few minutes before Jeff walked out with a bloody butcher knife. He didn't say anything. Megan held her breath and started to take Toni and run when he spoke.

"It's over... It's over this time, I'm sure of it. The bastard isn't breathing... and he has no pulse." Jared said as he held on to his girls.

Eight years later.

"Erin Goodman." The lady on the microphone called out.

Jared and Megan were attending Toni's high school graduation. Megan could only see the back of Toni's head, but could feel her smile. Toni had overcome so much with her years of therapy, struggling with her grades, falling into the wrong crowd and getting into drugs, but Toni really turned things around and was going to be attending a good college in the fall.

"Antonia Graham." The lady called out.

Megan and Jared rose to their feet with applause for their daughter. They sat back down and Megan wiped away a few tears of joy when she looked to her left and her heart almost stopped. Sitting four seats down from her was Toni. At least it was someone or something that looked exactly like Toni. She gasped and turned to Jared. That's when she noticed what she hadn't before. She knew by his stare and his blank expression. Those eyes. The past eight years she had not been living with the good Jared.

Read on for a sneak preview of

the first novel in my forthcoming

Agnes of Death book series.

Agnes of Death

The Mysterious man walked into the bar. It was a seedy looking

country and western style bar. There were 6 people congregated

around the bar and a forty something man playing pool and flirting

with a twenty something girl he had met hours ago. The mysterious man definitely didn't look like he belonged in this bar. He had a young look with his long dark hair, sunglasses and was wearing leather pants and a plain black t-shirt. He looked around the room at the lovely females and ran his tongue across his sharp fangs. He snapped his fingers suddenly and pointed in front of him. The bartender, who looked to be in her early thirties with shoulder length brown hair and a body that made most male patrons drool, leaped across the bar and ran to the side of the man. The lady sitting at the bar with her husband, who came here every Friday night, left his side and rushed to the opposite side of the man. He glanced over at the pool table where the young blonde girl was already en-route to him. She dropped to her knees and immediately began licking his black motorcycle boots.

The rotund man whose wife had left his side to be with the strange man stood up and angrily walked towards the man before turning to his wife.

"Terri, what the hell are you doing?" He yelled at her. She ignored him and continued to stare at the stranger while rubbing his body with her hands.

"Ask her that in about an hour." The man said.

"I wasn't talking to you freak!" He yelled at the man.

"You really do not want to fuck with me fat boy." The stranger said.

The man from the bar took a wild swing at the stranger, who promptly caught his fist in the palm of his hand and with one swift motion twisted his fist until his wrist popped. The rotund man fell to the floor clutching his hand and yelling out in pain.

"In case you were wondering my name is Daniel Darkholne." The strange man said. "I am new in town and just wanted to stop by for some entertainment for the evening."

He looked at the ladies and turned to walk away. Before he could reach the door he turned back.

"I almost forgot. I have my motorcycle with me. There is no way I can transport these lovely ladies back to my motel. If someone would kindly lend me a vehicle it would be greatly appreciated." He said.

Without hesitation, the man, who was still laying on the floor, released his clutch on his broken wrist long enough to retrieve the keys to his Chevy Blazer. He crawled across the floor to hand them to Darkholne.

"Thank you very much. I shall spare your life now." Darkholne said to the man whose wife he would be taking back to his motel room.

Three hours later Darkholne sat on the edge of the bed. He had been satisfied sexually by the three women and his thirst for blood had been satisfied as well. Normally he only feasted on one body but he had been fasting for a few days while traveling to this small western town known as Crow's Basin. He looked back at the three lifeless bodies of the women he had taken from the bar and smiled.

He felt fulfilled with his place in life and was happy he had allowed

a vampire to bite him, turning him into what he is today, one

hundred thirty six years ago.

Thanks for reading!

Be sure to check out my e-book short story series *The Z Word* and

my book of Horror/Comedy short stories *Stories That Should Not Be*

Told. Also coming soon, my new zombie apocalypse book *Weird*

Tales from Outcrop.

About the Author

Charles Riffle is a long-time horror fan who has been writing since childhood. He lives in a tiny town in West Virginia with his gorgeous wife, and their five rescue animals.

Printed in Great Britain
by Amazon